Lizza spread her hand over her heart.

"The love of your life is out there. I can just feel it. Right here. And Mr. Wonderful—that is, *your* Mr. Wonderful—is somewhere out there. Just waiting for you to dazzle his life. In fact, even as a little boy he was yearning for you, calling out to you—"

"Okay, you'd better quit while you're ahead." Nori smiled. "Where do you come up with this stuff, anyway?"

"I watch a lot of historical romances on cable." Lizza shrugged. "But I *did* mean what I said. *Your* Mr. Wonderful might live right here in Hot Springs. And he might be the next man who walks through that door."

The bell jingled over the door, making them both jump. Nori and Lizza stared at the front door.

Nori felt the hinge on her mouth let go. *I cannot believe this.* Zachary Martin, dressed in a cowboy hat and boots, stood in the doorway tipping his hat at her.

ANITA HIGMAN hopes to give her audience a "gasp and a giggle" when they read her stories. She's the award-winning author of eighteen books. Anita has a BA in speech communication and is a member of American Christian Fiction Writers. Anita enjoys hiking with her family, visiting show caves, and cooking brunch for her friends. Please drop by her book café for a cyber visit at www.anitahigman.com.

Books by Anita Higman

HEARTSONG PRESENTS
HP734—Larkspur Dreams (coauthored with Janice A. Thompson)
HP778—The Love Song (coauthored with Janice A. Thompson)

JANICE A. THOMPSON is a Christian author from Texas. She has four grown daughters, and the whole family is active in ministry, particularly the arts. Janice is a writer by trade but wears many other hats, as well. She previously taught drama and creative writing at a Christian school of the arts. She also directed a global drama missions team. She currently heads up the elementary department at her church and enjoys public speaking. Janice is passionate about her faith and does all she can to share it with others, which is why she particularly loves writing inspirational novels. Through her stories, she hopes to lead others into a relationship with a loving God.

Books by Janice A. Thompson

HEARTSONG PRESENTS
HP490—A Class of Her Own
HP593—Angel Incognito
HP613—A Chorus of One
HP666—Sweet Charity
HP677—Banking on Love
HP734—Larkspur Dreams (coauthored with Anita Higman)
HP754—Red Like Crimson
HP778—The Love Song (coauthored with Anita Higman)
HP786—White as Snow
HP806—Out of the Blue

Don't miss out on any of our super romances. Write to us at the following address for information on our newest releases and club information.

Heartsong Presents Readers' Service
PO Box 721
Uhrichsville, OH 44683

Or visit www.heartsongpresents.com

Castles in the Air

Anita Higman and Janice A. Thompson

Heartsong Presents

To the brave men and women of our United States military,
who stand in harm's way that we might enjoy the freedoms we hold dear.
A.H.

To Courtney and Andy—both sweeter than candy.
J.A.T.

ACKNOWLEDGMENTS:
Gratitude goes to my husband, Peter, for his boundless help and support.
A.H.

A note from the Author:
I love to hear from my readers! You may correspond with me by writing:

Anita Higman and Janice A. Thompson
Author Relations
PO Box 721
Uhrichsville, OH 44683

ISBN 978-1-60260-073-7

CASTLES IN THE AIR

Our mission is to publish and distribute inspirational products offering exceptional value and biblical encouragement to the masses.

PRINTED IN THE U.S.A.

one

The tiniest scream rose inside Nori. She tucked the desperate feeling away as she watched a cozy-looking duo through the coffee shop window. The pair held hands and kissed, making a tight little circle of love.

Not wanting to torture herself, Nori moved on down the sidewalk and turned her attention to a display window at Simon's Book Shoppe. A title on one of the covers grabbed her attention: *Guerrilla Tactics for the Romantically Challenged.* She shook her head in disbelief as another book title ground into her psyche: *Why You Aren't Dating—Put Down That Chocolate!*

Nori rolled her eyes and slipped the candy bar she'd been eating into her coat pocket. Apparently, the author was uninformed that the cocoa bean was good for the heart.

The last book in the display clutched at her heart. *When Love Never Comes.* How much more could she stand? She forced a chuckle, but somewhere deep inside, where little girls grow up dreaming of happily-ever-afters, she knew her aloneness was getting to her.

A tear spilled down Nori's cheek. She glanced around, embarrassed. Swiping at her eyes, she started her usual pep talk. *Remember who you are—a successful entrepreneur. The newspapers call you "The Candy Shop Queen."*

A gust of icy air nipped at Nori's exposed skin. It seemed extra cold for mid-March. She pulled her coat collar up around her neck and strode to her car.

Nori's pace slowed. She glanced back. What if one of the books had even one idea in it that could change her clichéd life? She'd be foolish *not* to buy it. Right? Desperate times—desperate measures.

Nori turned around, and before she could change her mind again, she charged into the bookstore. She drew in a deep breath. The shop smelled of peppermint and coffee.

"I'll be there in a minute," a women yoo-hooed from the back room.

Not wanting to be embarrassed with unnecessary queries, Nori reached around into the small window display and pulled out a book entitled, *Finding Your Dreamboat.* She hadn't noticed that one before. Hmm. The book might have potential, but the cover nearly screamed, "Find out now why the whole world considers you undatable."

She flipped open to the contents page and scanned it. The book appeared to be set up with long lists of ideas. *"Tip Number One: Surround yourself with romance. Talk romantically. Dress romantically. And the greatest secret of all is to—"*

"Excuse me," a stranger whispered in her ear.

Nori screamed. In that instant the book became airborne, ricocheted off some shelves, and made a nasty landing on the wooden floor.

"Mmm, so you're the anxious type." The woman raised one heavy eyebrow. "Oh, I see you have one of our newest arrivals." She scooped up the book and glared at the crushed corners.

"Don't worry," Nori said. "I'll buy it."

The bell over the door jangled, and a man with some serious good looks ambled inside. Lots of Grecian angles and lustrous hair with highlights. *The guy is prettier than I am.* He glanced over at Nori and caught her drooling.

"Gertrude!" The bushy-browed clerk hollered loud enough to summon emergency personnel. "Somebody just bought that how-to-trap-a-man book in the window. You know, *Finding Your Dreamboat.* Can you bring me up another copy?"

Nori wanted to crawl under something. She might as well slap on a sandwich board with the word *desperate* and strut all over Hot Springs. "Uh, maybe you could just put the book on hold for me," Nori whispered to the clerk as she edged toward the door.

"There's no waiting whatsoever. You can buy this one. Actually, you *should* buy this one since you mangled it."

She wondered what Mr. Dazzle thought about that announcement. Or maybe he hadn't been paying attention.

On her way up to pay, Nori noticed a coffee-table book on the art of making homemade Christmas candy. Maybe she could sell a selection of books in her candy shop. She scribbled a note on her hand to remind her.

Back at the counter, the clerk frowned at Nori's check. "I'll need to see an ID, please. I can't be too careful for Melody. I'm just helping her out tonight for a few minutes." She glanced at her watch. "In fact, I'd better get back. I really belong next door in the nut shop."

What more could Nori possibly add to that thoroughly accurate statement? She paid for the book, slapped on the sweetest smile she could conjure, and fled out the front door.

Ahh. The arctic air felt revitalizing. But as she took off toward her car, an age-old question came back to haunt her—was there really a man somewhere out there who was meant to love her? No answer whispered back to her in the cold evening wind. When had falling in love gotten so complicated? Her own parents had fallen in love and were still happy. And what about all those dear elderly couples at the assisted living center where she'd volunteered? They'd found soul mates and were blissfully growing old together.

Huge flakes floated down and lighted on Nori's face. She looked up. The thick clouds seemed expectant. Tonight she might choose to tuck herself in with a blanket of self-pity.

She knew a gloomy attitude wouldn't get her very far, but flying free from the constant yearning to have a family seemed nearly impossible.

In fact, she recalled the moment the seed was planted. Her mother had given her a wedding doll on her sixth birthday, and she playacted a hundred different kinds of weddings as she grew up. Breezy hilltop weddings. Cathedral weddings. Outdoor gazebo weddings. Then she'd create detailed lives for her lovebirds with careers and houses and kids. But sadly, her elaborate dreams were only built in her imagination. Only castles in the air.

She sighed. Life would be easier if her customers weren't escalating the situation by making suggestions. People tried to be helpful, but their encouragement and suggestions left a residue on her spirit, reminding her that she was on the spinster side of nuptial bliss. And that time was slipping away.

Nori scooted into her older model Mercedes and started the engine. As she waited for the heat, she looked into the rearview mirror. She touched the corners of her eyes. No wrinkles or sags. She hadn't turned into a gargoyle. Yet.

She leaned into the reflection. *Okay. Not bad at thirty.* Shoulder length, blond hair. A little washed-out, but all natural and no gray. Clear hazel eyes. Perfect oval face. None of that distracting bone structure like on magazine models. Surely she was still datable.

She knocked the mirror back in place. But she was still twenty pounds overweight. One of the hazards of loving dark chocolate truffles and owning the finest candy shop in Arkansas. Nori brushed at the bulging folds of fabric above her stomach as if to sweep them away. They'd been part of her life for ten years, so they weren't about to disappear overnight. But couldn't true love transcend a mere twenty pounds of flesh?

Nori looked out through the window across the empty parking lot and released a long breath. She wondered if God had taken notice that her sighing had recently increased. Did He keep a count of people's sighs and tears as He did the hairs on their heads?

God, I know You're listening, so here I am yet again with some more questions. Am I still going to be kissing the mirror when I'm creaking with arthritis? You've crowned me the princess of the friendship date. In all these years I have never even had a kiss I could call a real kiss. Only lips brushing across a cheek and little pecks on the forehead. I want a big juicy kiss! Can I say that to You, God? And I want our passionate kiss to mean something. Something real and lasting. A forever kind of kiss. And God. . .if it's not too much to ask. . .the next wedding I attend, I'd like it to be mine.

Silence. Seemed like there'd been a lot of that lately, too. Or maybe God wasn't saying what she wanted to hear.

Suddenly Nori noticed that Mr. Dazzle from the bookstore was trotting in her direction. She leaned in toward the windshield for a better look. Could the book have worked its magic by merely purchasing it? Or was the guy going to try to steal her car?

The stranger came toward her waving a book in his hands. Nori saw her purse on the passenger seat—no book. *Oh, great.* She'd left her purchase sitting on the counter. Mr. Dazzle had her book. Nori let her head fall forward against the steering wheel as she closed her eyes. *Is there no end to my humiliation?*

two

Nori looked up to see the stranger's knuckles about to give her window a rap. She pushed a button on the side panel. The glass glided downward as she looked up at him, feeling grateful that the shadows of the car hid her embarrassment. "Hi, there."

He offered her the book. "You forgot this."

She tried to swallow her pride, but it felt as pleasant as gulping down a walnut. Unshelled. She reached out through the window for the book. "I really appreciate it."

A tiny cross swung around his neck on a silver chain. "Good luck," he said.

"Excuse me?" Nori felt her heart do a little two-step.

"You know," he said. "Good luck finding your dreamboat."

Okay, so how many shades of embarrassment are there? Flaming scarlet. Lobster-pink. Fuchsia fandango. Nori released a nervous giggle. "Thanks."

"It took me two years to find mine," he went on to say. "I'd recommend starting with a sailboat if you like adventure. Nothing else like it. Leave your cares behind." He appeared sincere.

And people have the nerve to make fun of female blondes.

"Yeah, I got a great deal on Serendipity. It's the name of my boat." He flashed his pearly whites as he flipped his collar-length hair back. "I found her in the newspaper. Sort of an unforeseen blessing. By the way, I'm Blake Lawrence."

She shook his warm hand. "I'm Nori Kelly. It's nice to meet you."

10

He paused for a moment as if wanting to ask her something. Then the moment dissipated along with the cloud from his frosty breath. "Well, I guess I'd better get going. It's pretty cold out here." He stomped around as he blew into his hands. "Hey, look, it's snowing. Now that's a surprise."

Nori stared upward and saw a few large and lacy flakes float around him. The snow had started sputtering again. "Yeah, life is full of surprises."

Blake chuckled as he looked at her. He stuck his hands into the pockets of his leather jacket. "Take care, now. Okay?"

"You, too."

Mr. Dazzle bowed like a nobleman and then bid her adieu.

Nori watched the man walk away. Blinking a few more times, she tried to take it all in. *That was different.* She rubbed her hands but realized she was already warm. She paused for another moment or two and then sped off toward her apartment, grateful for a cozy place to be lonely and crazy. But she had to admit, the man tonight was not only cute but friendly. And she was glad he hadn't "gotten it." Otherwise the moment would have been awkward instead of sweet.

Hmm. Too bad Blake hadn't been in the mood to buy her some cocoa in the nearby coffee shop. Cocoa reigned supreme as the beverage of choice for a snowy evening, especially with those soft marshmallows bobbing their little heads around on top. Oh yes, mocha moo in a mug. The brew should be savored around stimulating conversation, but if alone, a book and a cup of the sweet charm could always be her escape and comfort. And a man who took the time to appreciate cocoa was a man worth taking another look at.

Blake Lawrence. Too bad. Nice name. Sounded a little fake, like a character from a romance novel, but nice anyway. Well, if there'd been an opportunity in that brief moment, it was gone now.

Nori started singing anything that came into her head—anything to get her mind off her spiraling thoughts. She was still humming when she parked her car, rode the elevator to the second floor of her apartment building, and strode down the hallway to her front door.

Oh no. She noticed her neighbor, Zachary Martin, emerge from his apartment as if he'd been waiting for her.

"Greetings." He appeared to study the floor.

"Hi." Nori wondered why Zachary was the only one in the known galaxy to greet people that way.

He raked his fingers through his short brown hair, which made a couple of his locks rise up like antlers.

Nori squelched a chuckle. She knew he was stalling, trying to think of something to say. If she hadn't been so tired, she would have given him a few rounds of chitchat. Instead she jangled her keys to give him a hint.

Zachary stuffed his fists in his pockets, making his polyester pants rise even higher. His white socks emitted a glow as if lit by a black light. "Hope your evening has been. . .good. . .so far."

"I think it has been. . .so far." Nori smiled, sliding her key into the lock.

"The National Oceanic and Atmospheric Administration says there's a 20 percent chance of snow tonight." Zachary stroked his palms together.

"It's already snowing." Nori tried not to have a condescending tone.

He shuffled his feet. "Oh."

Nori turned her door key. She didn't want to be rude, but her feet throbbed from working all day. "I've been out window-shopping this evening," she said, trying to throw him a preserver so he wouldn't drown in their silence.

Zachary puckered his eyebrows. "I do that all the time, too. Well, I window-shop. . .online." He snickered.

When she didn't respond with laughter, he recoiled as if to censor himself. *I think I was supposed to laugh.* Nori felt sorry for Zachary. He'd been her neighbor for a whole year, and yet they'd never once connected even as friends.

Zachary shrugged with his palms in the air.

Nori noticed the ink scribblings on his hand. He apparently had the same habit of writing notes on his hand as she did.

Silence crawled between them again—the prickly kind.

These gawking and quiet elements of his personality made Nori nervous. Plus his body gestures made her think of Mr. Potato Head when some of the parts were put back wrong. She certainly wasn't up for the stress of jump-starting their weekly hall conversations. "Well, I guess I'd better go on in." She opened her door and waved. "Good night."

"Sure. Thanks for talking to me. . .Noreen."

Nori paused and then turned to him again. "I do wish you'd call me Nori. The name *Noreen* makes me feel old."

"Noreen Kelly is an Irish name." Zachary had a faraway gaze. "From the land of flaming dragons and fair maidens," he added with a brogue.

Nori tried not to look too baffled.

"Oh. It's from a fantasy trilogy I've been reading. It's set in Ireland. You know, Land of the Flaming Dragons." Zachary stuck his elbow out as if to lean against the door frame, but his aim was so off, he stumbled and fell against the wall.

"Are you okay?" Nori wanted to help him, but he'd already grabbed the door frame and pulled himself up.

"Yeah." He raised his arms. "I'm good."

"Are you sure?"

He nodded, his face red. "Yep."

"Well, okay. Good-bye." Nori glanced back.

She caught him mouthing, "Good night." He said nothing more, so she smiled and eased the door shut.

Once inside her cocoon, Nori busied herself by hanging up her coat in the entry closet, but her thoughts remained on Zachary. Had she been unsociable? Perhaps. Here was a guy who'd actually showed some real interest, and she'd shut him out. Maybe she was being too picky. But she had hoped for a partner who was in the same species. *Oh dear.* Guilt clouded over Nori like the murky sky outside. She sent up a sincere apology to God, grabbed her teddy bear, and plopped down on her overstuffed couch with a sigh.

Zachary wasn't so bad. Really. A handsome face when he didn't scowl. He had quite a mannish body, but the clothing could use some work. Same age and height as her—thirty and short. And on more than one occasion he'd mentioned how much he loved his church. All in all, he appeared to be a kind and thoughtful Christian man. That all rang up well. But one iffy issue really stood out—Zachary was a geek.

But then again, Nori reminded herself, she'd also had some endearing moments with him. Zachary never looked through her as so many other men did. He took the time to listen to her—to really "see" her. She wondered if there wasn't something about him undiscovered or perhaps misunderstood by people. Something one had to quietly seek, instead of just tossing out quick assumptions and dismissals. Had she been guilty of the latter? She gave her teddy a squeeze.

Nori ambled over to the kitchen counter with her bear, trying to imagine herself falling in love with someone like that. She wondered what he did in his cave with all his alone time. Just read medieval fantasy novels and play with his calculator? Sounded boring. She hardly ever heard a peep from his apartment next door. *What is he doing right this minute?* Funny how she'd never thought about that before, and he'd been next door for about a year.

What would her parents think of Zachary? Nori chuckled.

They would like him. They'd adore anyone who'd marry her. Oh well, things to muse about some other day.

Nori reached down into one of her sample bags sitting on the counter and popped a few of the new chocolate-covered raisins into her mouth. Fine dark chocolate with a hint of orange. Mmm. Okay, this would sell to all of those female customers, including herself, who loved specialty chocolates almost as much as a good date. Almost.

She'd need to order some of the new treats but not without first allowing her best customers to sample them and decide. With no paper handy, she wrote out the reminder on the palm of her hand. She'd transfer the note to her memo pad later. Hmm. Maybe what she really needed were some hobbies beyond sampling chocolates. She chuckled. All her extra time went into the candy shop, so it had seemed almost impossible to explore any leisure pursuits.

Nori's gaze latched onto the slick hardbound book she'd just bought. *Finding Your Dreamboat.* Ignoring the almost condescending book title, she scooted the book closer and then cracked it opened in the middle as if some magical air might escape. The thirteenth chapter began: *"Makeup is an essential. Your skin is like a primer coat, so don't forget the paint. Without color, you're like a rose without its petals."*

"That's ridiculous," Nori mumbled. "I've never needed more than blush." She pulled up the sleeves on her turtleneck sweater. Out of curiosity, she read on: *"Try wearing liberal amounts of lipstick in the hue of pomegranates. Men are attracted to this ruby color—the color of ardor and romance. You don't need to flirt. Let your lips do it for you."*

Nori laughed. *Is this a joke?* But in spite of her doubts, she headed to the bathroom and rummaged through her makeup drawer for the tube of lipstick someone had given her for Christmas. The bottom of the tube read "Carnival of Rubies."

Hmm. Well, that name certainly didn't inspire confidence. She rolled up the lipstick from the container. Amazingly, it looked pretty close to the color of pomegranates, but once she smoothed it all over her lips, "Carnival of Circus Clowns" came to mind. *Oh dear.* "So much for desperate times— desperate measures." In an effort to attract males, she'd become no more than some animal preening her plumage. Nori released a prolonged sigh.

She set the gold case down on the counter and puckered her lips. Well, at least it was a *new* look. She decided she'd go ahead and give the fruity, flirty lip color a try the next morning. Besides, nothing else had worked. So what did she have to lose?

three

After pacing the halls trying to think of impressive things to say to Nori in the future, Zachary retreated to his apartment and eased his front door shut. He let his head fall against the wall in frustration. He knew that gently thumping his head against the Sheetrock was futile, not to mention juvenile, but it felt good for some reason. Why had he acted so absurdly in front of her? In trying to kid around, he'd had some kind of intellectual blackout.

Hearing a crinkling in his pocket, he reached in and yanked out his latest paycheck from South Gate Oil and Gas. He slung it into a drawer in the entry table. He had more money than he could spend, but it couldn't buy him what he really wanted— the love of his life, Noreen Kelly. The woman had everything. Good teeth. Brains. A Mona Lisa smile.

Ah yes, his Nori was as fair as any maiden he'd ever read about. And sometimes when he got lost in her smile, he'd come close to just reaching out and touching her face without thinking.

In fact, he could easily recall the moment he'd fallen in love with her. One evening after work when he'd stopped in to buy his favorite candy, Nori was holding a baby girl while her mother shopped. She cuddled and sang to the child about Jesus until both Nori and the baby took on the most angelic countenances he'd ever beheld. He'd known in that moment he was smitten—for life.

Zachary groaned. Such amorous sentiments, and he couldn't even summon the courage to ask her out. He knew he lacked certain social skills, but he didn't need any coaching to see Noreen had "no" written all over her face. At least now he knew to always call her *Nori* in the future, since she seemed to dislike her given name. He couldn't understand why, though, since her full name made a sound as melodic as water gurgling over stones and moss.

After squeezing the bridge of his nose and adjusting his glasses, he glanced around. At least his domicile wasn't holding him back from settling down. His dwelling looked like a class act with all its contemporary furniture and technology. He had plenty of food, a more than comfortable income, and an expensive apartment. Of course, wooing was more than just dangling possessions in front of a woman, he reminded himself, but his financial status wouldn't hurt his chances.

Zachary gave a light whack to the model of the solar system sitting on the table. He liked the peculiar whirring noise it created. He watched the tiny planets lose their order as they flew out of control.

Maybe he still lacked some piece of the puzzle. He'd always been good at figuring things out, and now as a grown man, he certainly knew about geophysical interpretations, computer analysis, and physical models. But love and the female psyche seemed impossible to decode. In fact, no real solution came to him because there were no right answers.

Lost in thought, Zachary lumbered over to his telescope and touched the eyepiece. He wondered if Galileo had gone through as much trouble wooing a girl. Flustered, he dismissed the subject and stumbled into the kitchen to make a homemade cup of cocoa.

Once he had the brew poured into his cup from the pan, he took a cautious sip of his concoction. The heady steam curled upward and calmed him. *Good stuff.* Just the way his dad used to make it. "Top secret ingredients," his dad used to say with a wink. Dark chocolate and marshmallow cream. Those days seemed like an eternity ago—when his parents were still together. But those times were gone now, and he'd moved on.

An Irish tune came to him, and, wanting to be free of the melancholy, he made an instrument out of his spoon and began clinking it against the cup to the rhythm in his head. When the song played itself out, he picked up his new calculator and began fiddling with it. He already had three on his desk at work, but the new one could do three-dimensional graphics. Well worth the money. If only love could be as simple as an equation.

Zachary glanced up at the book he'd bought at Simon's Book Shoppe the day before and crossed his arms. *Courtship for Idiots.* He'd circled the aisles in the bookstore about fifty times before he bolstered his nerve to buy the thing. Now it sat there on the shelf, face forward and almost sneering at him.

He picked up the book and read the endorsements on the back: *"I found my wife with the advice from this book. What better endorsement is there?" "These ideas will change the course of your life. Buy it now, and let the journey begin."*

Zachary wondered if the overly glowing plugs were just made up by the author or submitted by close family and friends. He opened the book to the table of contents. It seemed to be set up under character types. "Teaching the Shy Guy to Say Hi." "Bob, the Pompous Snob." "Let's Meet the Freaky Geek."

Before scanning the next chapter titles, Zachary flipped to the geek chapter out of curiosity. He frowned and then read on: *"If you live in geekdom, your first task toward balance is to expand your reading materials to something besides technical journals."* He certainly wasn't guilty of falling into that trap, since he also loved reading science fiction and fantasy.

Zachary skimmed the author's reading list suggestions and then read a passage out loud. " 'Here are two more starter survival tactics. Pitch, cut up, or flush those nerdy white socks. And drive your shirts to the dry cleaners so they don't make you look like you slept in a dumpster.' "

He scooted his chair back to stare at his white socks. *Humph.* But white socks could be bought in big packages like bulk toilet paper. It was much more economical and logical to buy socks that way. And laundries were for sissies. He looked at his shirt. Not many wrinkles. Was it really necessary to iron clothes? They seemed to come out of the dryer sort of ready to wear. Didn't they?

He slapped the book shut in irritation and then took another sip of his cocoa. *Geekdom?* He wasn't truly a geek. Granted, he'd been called that term from time to time, but he'd never acknowledged it. He read the next sentence out loud. " 'You may be in denial.' "

Shocked, Zachary dropped the book as if he'd been electrocuted. After pacing the room, he finally picked it up again to take another peek. He read:

"If you're in denial, don't fret. Just acknowledge your status as a communal outcast and then take heart. Geeks also control some serious cash, because of their superior brain power. That counts for a lot more than the guy down the street who has more hair-care products than brain cells. With your keen intellect, you'll catch on faster when it comes to tweaking the persona. So let's get started."

Zachary knew the book was idiotic, but the bright spot of encouragement egged him on to the next page. " 'Okay, listen up. Another news flash. Women don't like guys who wear thick glasses. Get contacts. You can afford them.'" He pulled down his glasses and rubbed the bridge of his nose. He'd worn eyeglasses all his life. They'd become like an appendage to his face. He wasn't even sure if he could let go of them. Then he thought of lovely Nori again. He pushed his glasses back up and vowed to make an eye doctor's appointment for contacts.

Okay. What could possibly be next? Zachary read on, " 'Women like the unexpected. In other words, if you're a geek, consider each thing you do and then do the exact opposite. Think *surprise*.'"

Could he really make all these modifications? Or would he always be a communal outcast, as the book implied? And why had God made him so different?

ə.

After a weird night of wrestling with the sheets and dreaming he was Gollum in *The Lord of the Rings*, Zachary woke up with a wicked cramp in his neck and still very much in love with Nori Kelly.

Zachary threw on his robe and staggered into the kitchen, where he gobbled down his usual frosted peanut butter protein bar, three jumbo prunes, and one half-liter of hazelnut coffee. After showering, he climbed into the pair of khaki pants that he usually saved for church and put on his only unwrinkled shirt.

While fumbling in his closet, he came across a chunky bottle of cologne that his parents had given him when he was a teenager. Except for deodorant, he'd never taken the time to use anything with a scent.

Hmm. New territory. Zachary gave the bottle a dubious look. Surely he could handle it. The name of the cologne was Legends. Sounded pretty decent. Of course, bad things became legends, too.

Zachary shook the bottle, making the amber liquid slosh around in the container. How much of this stuff was he supposed to use anyway? Since he had no idea, he just opened his shirt and splashed a generous amount of the fluid all over his chest.

Then he gagged. *Way too much.* Zachary grabbed a washcloth, soaped it up, and tried scrubbing off the scent. But the smell seemed to be embedded in his skin. Permanently.

After a few more frustrating attempts at improving himself, Zachary gave up and waited by the front door. He smashed his ear against the wood, waiting for the sound of Nori as she left her apartment. She always made the same noises. He knew them by heart. She always locked the door, zipped up her purse, sighed, and then exactly five seconds later she'd come back to make sure she'd locked it. It was yet another connection he had with his Irish maiden. They were both serious checkers.

Yes, he heard the click, zip, and then her stride back to the door. His cue. Zachary exited, minus his white socks and rumpled clothes. With the new mantra buzzing in his head, he smiled over at Nori.

Remember, "Women like the unexpected. Consider each thing you do and then do the opposite. Think surprise."

four

Nori checked the door to make sure it was locked. Then she heard Zachary coming out of his apartment. *Oh no.* How did he always know when she left? He was like a human motion detector. She looked down the hall at him. "Hi."

"Good morning, Nori." Zachary smiled, and then without another word, he headed down the hallway toward the elevator, a book tightly clutched in his hand.

Hmm. That was different. Nori followed Zachary at a safe distance, looking him over. Something had changed about him. He didn't look so desperate or pitiful. And his clothes weren't crumpled. But what was that smell he left in his wake? After another whiff she realized "herbicide" might be a better word.

Ivan Wentworth, another bachelor apartment dweller, joined Nori and Zachary on their march down the hallway.

"Hi, Ivan," Nori said, trying not to be too obnoxious by puckering her lips.

"Morning." And then Ivan went back to talking into his earpiece.

Zachary turned to give Ivan a little wave but kept walking.

After they all boarded the elevator, Nori went up and down on her tiptoes, hoping someone, anyone, had noticed her lips. She had indeed decided to wear two layers of pomegranate lipstick. Even though Ivan was now off the phone, unfortunately he'd soon busied himself by fiddling with his PDA. And Zachary, who never read in the elevator, had his nose buried in a book. *So much for letting one's lips do the flirting.*

The elevator doors slid open, and the two men fled as if they were in a foot-race.

Nori stood gaping, wondering why men were so unpredictable. And scattered. And insensitive. In fact, a long list of vivid adjectives came to mind. What a farce.

Zachary popped his head around the elevator door and offered her a tissue. "I noticed your lip was bleeding. Hope you're okay."

Nori accepted the neatly folded tissue. She opened her mouth to speak, but Zachary disappeared around the corner. She mashed her floor button a few times, rode the elevator back to her apartment, and stared at herself in the bathroom mirror. The lip color had smeared under her mouth, making her lip appear cut and bleeding. In fact, the sticky crimson goo had also gotten on her teeth, which made her look like she'd been hanging out with vampires. The color of romance, indeed.

After cleaning herself up and starting the day again, she drove over to her shop. She swung open the door and took in the aroma of every kind of wonderful treat. Sweet Nothings Candy Shop—her dream come to life. A quaint sign swung over the door, a black-and-white checkered floor lit the store with pizzazz, and magic waited in every jar of candy. *Ah yes*.

She lighted her fingers on some dainty bags of her famous Little Chocola' Rocks. *Mmm, mmm, mmm.* How could men compete with sweets, especially chocolate? She chuckled to herself.

Lizza Langtree, her manager, effervescent as always, stood behind the counter in her rainbow overalls schmoozing the customers until they were all helplessly buying several kinds of candies. A mom and her giggling children strolled out with a diverse assortment of goodies—watermelon worms, which were all the rage with the kids; homemade maple walnut fudge, good for buttering up dads; and the delectable caramel chews, which were a superb choice for apple-dipping even though the time for autumn treats had passed.

"Hey, girl." Lizza gave Nori a hug.

"Looks like you're already busy satisfying our tourists this morning." Nori hugged her back. Lizza had always been big on hugs. Even with her slender frame, she'd mastered the big bear squeeze.

After they discussed the inventory for Mother's Day, Nori tied on her rainbow apron over her navy pantsuit and did her usual round of cleaning.

Two hours later, Nori changed out some of the candies in the display window while Lizza refilled a few of the candy bins. "You know, you can handle the store so well, I barely even need to show up."

"Now aren't you glad you hired me?" Lizza turned around and winked at Nori. "It was a good day, wasn't it. . .the day I came to work for you?" She raised her hand for a high five, her blue eyes twinkling.

"Best day of my life." Nori slapped Lizza's hand and chuckled. Lizza loved high fives almost as much as bear hugs.

"I still can't believe your grandmother gave you the money to start this place. My grandma doesn't even bake me cookies."

Nori grinned. "Well, Grandma Essie didn't bake me cookies either, but she did believe in my dream. While I got my business degree, Grandma knew I wanted to own a candy shop someday. So when I graduated, this was my present."

"You gotta love that. Talk about faith in your granddaughter."

"Yeah, and I will be forever grateful." Nori remembered her grandma's pep talks and her letters of encouragement. "Grandma never wanted me to do all the work by myself. She said she was afraid I'd burn out. You see, Grandma believed in my dream, but she was also desperate for great-grandchildren.

Since I was the only one who could give them to her, she was hoping I'd use my surplus time to find a husband and have babies." Nori sighed.

"Too bad she went to heaven before she saw you married."

"Well, even if Grandma *had* lived, there was no guarantee that she was ever going to see me get married."

Lizza spread her hand over her heart. "The love of your life is out there. I can just feel it. Right here. And Mr. Wonderful—that is, *your* Mr. Wonderful—is somewhere out there. Just waiting for you to dazzle his life. In fact, even as a little boy he was yearning for you, calling out to you—"

"Okay, you'd better quit while you're ahead." Nori smiled. "Where do you come up with this stuff, anyway?"

"I watch a lot of historical romances on cable." Lizza shrugged. "But I *did* mean what I said. *Your* Mr. Wonderful might live right here in Hot Springs. And he might be the next man who walks through that door."

The bell jingled over the door, making them both jump. Nori and Lizza stared at the front door.

Nori felt the hinge on her mouth let go. *I cannot believe this.* Zachary Martin, dressed in a cowboy hat and boots, stood in the doorway tipping his hat at her.

"Now there's an interesting-looking man for you." Lizza looked back at Nori and made a lasso circle with her finger. "Yee-hah," she whispered. "Wait a minute. I recognize that guy. Isn't he your next-door neighbor? He's the one who comes in for chocolate-covered coffee beans."

"Yeah, he's a real candy lover," Nori said out of the corner of her mouth.

"Well, I've never said this, but I think he's cute. And—"

Nori placed two fingers over her own lips and pinched them together, trying to give Lizza the hint to be quiet. Fortunately, it didn't appear Zachary had heard them since he was busy bumping into things. *Must be because he forgot to put on his glasses.*

Zachary leaned over, checking out a silver tray of samples. He made one of his obscure hand gestures and then stared at the pastel mint candies as if he had them under a microscope.

Nori thought he said "Nice," as he tossed a handful of mints, one by one, into his mouth.

"Hi." Nori strolled toward him. "Did you come in for a little dessert?"

Zachary didn't reply. Instead, panic washed over his face. His hands grasped his throat as his face turned dark red. And then blue.

"Hey, he's choking!" Lizza screamed.

Nori looked at Lizza and then back at Zachary. His hands still clutched his neck.

Heimlich. Now. Nori got behind Zachary and threw her arms around his middle. She clasped her hands together in a ball and gave Zachary's chest a firm thrust with her fists. Nothing happened.

"Lower," Lizza yelled. "Move your hands down!"

Nori slid her hands downward and gave Zachary another hard push. A small round piece of mint sailed out of his mouth. In the midst of the drama, his hat flew off and tumbled across the floor.

Zachary gasped for air and coughed a few times. Then he leaned over with his hands on his knees.

Must be trying to get his bearings. Nori patted his back and breathed a prayer of thanksgiving.

Zachary sucked in some more air and then looked at Nori. "This isn't what. . ." His face flushed crimson.

"Are you okay now? I can't believe I almost killed you with my mints." Nori wanted to make him laugh, but she realized her comment might have come off clumsy.

Lizza rushed over and hugged Zachary. "I'm Lizza Langtree, by the way." She released him from her hold. "I'm glad you're alive."

"Me, too." he gave her a half smile. "I'm Zachary Martin."

Lizza shook his hand.

Zachary turned his attention to Nori. "You saved my life. Thank you."

"I would have done it for anyone." *Oh, that didn't come out right either.* "Please choose anything in the store. The candy is on the house." Nori certainly didn't want her customer and neighbor to go away unhappy. "Please tell me, what would you like?"

Zachary brightened. A little. "I'd like some. . .well, I'm addicted to. . .chocolate-covered coffee beans."

"Milk, dark, or extra dark?"

"I think I'll have dark today. Thanks."

"Good choice. Coming right up."

"Really appreciate. . .you know." Zachary opened his mouth to speak and then shook his head. He seemed to be holding a conversation with himself in his head.

Nori shoveled a few large scoops of her best beans into a clear plastic bag. *That should take care of him for a week or two.* She tied up the bag with a twist tie and handed it to him with a smile.

"Thanks. I hope you have a good life. I mean. . .you know. . . a good weekend." And with those rather uninspiring yet seemingly genuine words, Zachary went out the door.

Nori just stood there for a moment, absorbing the situation. She wasn't sure what just happened, except that Zachary had choked on one of her candies. Pretty terrible stuff. *I mean, what if he'd died?* She decided not to chase that thought too far. She took in several deep breaths to calm her heartbeat.

Then Nori suddenly wondered why Zachary had been

wearing a Western outfit. Was it somehow for her benefit? But sometimes he seemed more irritated around her than romantic, so what was up with that? She shook her head, feeling totally clueless, but so glad she was able to save his life.

"Oh man, I'm sure glad the shop was empty." Lizza blew a strand of hair off her face. "Your neighbor looks like he might not recover from that kind of embarrassment."

"How true."

Lizza tied another peach satin ribbon around a miniature box of gumdrops. "Zachary seems like a lonely guy. Makes me want to bundle him up and stick him in my pocket for safekeeping."

"Yeah, maybe." Nori helped Lizza stack the dainty boxes on a display table.

"I don't know. I always say that about people who look sort of lost. Like he doesn't know the secret."

"What secret?" Nori asked.

"That every person is wondrously hand-designed by God. I think the reason people don't turn out so well sometimes is because no one has ever told them that."

Nori thought if she told Zachary that he was wondrous, he would never stop pestering her. Hmm. But *was* he bothering her? She no longer knew for sure. In fact, this time she'd felt nervous and tongue-tied.

"And like I said, I think he's charming." Lizza gave the top box a little pat.

"He usually wears glasses, so I'd never noticed his eyes before. They're nice." Nori realized she was thinking out loud. The disclosure surprised her.

"Yes, they *were* nice eyes. And I think the real reason he came in was to ask you out. But he was too busy choking to death." Lizza winked.

"Please don't say that. I feel terrible as it is." Nori shook her head and grinned at Lizza. "And I don't think he came in to ask me out."

"Isn't that a bit negative?"

Nori placed her hands on her hips. "At *my* age, I'm just being realistic."

"Hey, don't say it like that. We're about the same age." Lizza jigged her eyebrows. "So, you're interested in him after all."

"He's not my type. He's a very nice nerd. But even though I'm lonely sometimes and I'd like to start a family before I buy nursing home insurance, I don't want to spend the rest of my life having one-sided discussions about quantum physics."

Lizza leaned back on the counter and whistled. "Where on earth did you get such a gloomy view of nerds? Haven't you heard? They rule the world."

Before Nori could answer, a teenage boy opened the door. He had a smart-alecky grin on his face and a ferret sitting on his shoulder.

"Hey, buddy, he's cute, but we don't allow zebras or ferrets in the shop," Lizza said to the kid. "They just can't stop eating the licorice."

The boy rolled his eyes and then headed back down the sidewalk. The moment he disappeared, lightning flashed outside the window. Thunder exploded through the shop, making the lids on the candy jars rattle.

Lizza chuckled. "Wow, that came out of nowhere."

"We've certainly had some unexpected storms lately." Nori shivered.

Then, like the thunder, Zachary burst back into the shop.

five

"Forgot something." Zachary snatched his hat off the floor and then shuffled out before Nori could say anything to him.

"Mmm. That's what I love about the candy business." Lizza's mouth curved up at the corners. "Never a dull moment."

My, my, my. I will never understand that guy. Nori squeezed the top of her head, wondering if she had a headache coming on.

Lizza massaged Nori's neck and shoulders as she whistled a Broadway tune. "You know, girl, there's no reason why you shouldn't have dates. *I* have dates."

"That's because you're gorgeous," Nori said. "You have sassy, short blond hair, cobalt blue eyes, and baby-soft skin. You're thin, you dress like a model, and you always have that smirk that must drive men crazy."

Lizza laughed. "Well, I wouldn't know about that." She released Nori with a pat on the back.

"Thanks." Nori scrunched up her shoulders. "That feels a lot better."

"Good," Lizza said. "Now, you want some free advice?"

"I can't guarantee I'll use it."

"Fair enough." Lizza got in front of Nori and caught her gaze. "If I come off pretty in any way, I have to give some credit to God and to. . .well. . .good makeup."

"You don't wear a lot of makeup."

"Yes, I do. You should see my bathroom cabinets and counters. I'll show you sometime. The trick with makeup is patience. You know, figuring out your best colors. How to apply it right. It takes some practice."

31

"Practice?" Nori raised an eyebrow. "Like rowing a boat or playing the clarinet?"

"Yeah, like anything you want to be good at. Why don't you get one of those free makeovers at the cosmetics counter at the mall?"

"Hmm."

"And. . .now this I would only say to someone I love."

"Oh no." Nori scrunched up her face. "Something bad. Right?"

"No, not *too* bad. Look, for some reason your dear mother didn't tell you to straighten your shoulders when you were a girl."

"I slump?"

"Yes, you do. It makes you come off as if you don't have any confidence, which couldn't be further from the truth. And I think you'd enjoy using that gym membership you bought."

"I'm chubby?" Why had it come out as a question? Nori was more than aware of her elephantine frame.

"You just need to tone up your softness a little."

Nori laughed. "I'm chubby. You can say it." She took in a deep breath and thought about all the advice. "I suppose there is some merit to your suggestions." She stared at the tiny boxes of chocolate-covered strawberries. She'd always taken great care that the fruits were fresh and sweet. Then she'd dip each ripe berry in the finest chocolate with a drizzle of white. "Perhaps I've taken more care with my candies than I have with myself."

"Tragic. Perhaps someone forgot to tell *you* the secret, too. You know, that God made every person wondrous."

Nori straightened her shoulders and smiled. "Perhaps."

A man strolled by the shop. Lizza and Nori both stopped to watch him stare at the treats in the window.

"Wow. Will you just look at that? I didn't think men were made that way anymore." Lizza shook her head with a dreamy expression. "He's like Adam coming out from the Garden of Eden. . .well, with clothes on."

"What do you think he's staring at in the window? I'll bet he's wanting to soften up Eve with a box of those pralines. She's mad because he wouldn't let her name any of the animals."

Lizza chuckled. "Good guess, but no cigar. Look at those worry lines around his brow. He's troubled because his mother's in the hospital with inoperable bunions, and he thinks some old-fashioned divinity would cheer her up."

"No way."

Before they could continue their game, the subject of their musings suddenly popped his head in the door and yelled, "Hey, do you all carry any canine treats? I'm looking for puppy truffles for my sheepdog."

six

Zachary trudged to his office. He took off his cowboy hat and stomped on it until it was no more than a horizontal piece of brown felt and a very bad memory.

He dropped into his chair and let his head slump down on his desk. The thud rocked his skull, but the sound was a relief compared to the screaming accusations in his head. How many things had gone wrong? *Let me count the ways.* Besides nearly choking to death, why had he bought those stupid clothes? Nori hadn't said a word about his attire. Likely she was too embarrassed for him and didn't want to add to his humiliation.

And that would be the last time he'd try to be *so* impulsive. Perhaps the book on courtship had good ideas, but when most men hear "surprise," they think about flowers. He'd somehow convinced himself that dressing differently would get Nori's attention. In a good way.

He lifted his aching head. But foolish as it was, in spite of the day's tragedy, he still wouldn't mind wandering back to the candy shop on his lunch break. Not just for his favorite candies. . .but to take another glimpse at the sweetest woman who ever lived.

Zachary swiveled around and stared at his computer screen, but his mind wouldn't let go of his disgrace he'd just suffered. The outfit had not only been a failure, but he'd come off as helpless instead of manly. In fact, Nori had been forced to save his pathetic life. Not very romantic.

Okay, repeat. I have an IQ of 160, so I'm not an idiot. I have an IQ of 160, so I'm not an idiot. Still, he felt like one. After all, he'd barely managed to speak a sensible word to Nori.

Wade, a coworker, strolled into Zachary's office. "Hey, how's it going?"

"Well, I'm here." Zachary rubbed his head.

"Women problems, eh, my man?" Wade eased his portly frame into one of Zachary's chairs, making its wooden limbs moan with what sounded like dread.

"How did you know that?" Wade had some bizarre intuitive thing going. He always popped in, made offhanded and wild speculations, and then usually guessed right. The encounters were starting to annoy Zachary.

"You looked kind of miserable. Had to be a woman."

"Right."

"How true," Wade said. "I *am* always right."

While Zachary waited for his coworker to leave, he straightened the items on his desk for the thousandth time. Fortunately Wade didn't notice his obsessive-compulsive disorder, since he was too busy combing and smoothing his thick mustache into what looked like an otter pelt.

His coworker appeared to be settling in for a while, so Zachary decided to ask, "You're happily married. So how did you get your wife to like you?"

Wade laughed. "Well, you can't *make* them like you. But it'd be so much simpler that way, wouldn't it?" He laughed. "I do have one secret, though."

Did he really want to know? "Oh yeah? What's that?"

"I softened Hallie up before I asked her out."

Zachary pulled back. *Yeah, you're a real Mr. Smooth.* "So, how did you soften her up?"

"I dazzled Hallie with surprises." He lifted the lid off Zachary's candy jar and helped himself to several wrapped chocolates.

"I'm afraid surprises have been my undoing," Zachary hoped Wade wouldn't slip half the jar of chocolates into his pocket like the last time. Good thing he didn't know about his private stash. "So what did you do?"

"Well, I found out Hallie liked Shakespeare, so I bought her the complete works bound in leather. And then on another week, I sent flowers anonymously."

"But what if she didn't know who sent them? Somebody else could get the credit."

"Risk, my man. That's what it takes." Wade laced his fingers together over his stomach. "Love is like radioactivity. In other words, unstable atoms decaying randomly."

Zachary winced. Well, *that* certainly sounded like the stuff romantic legends were made of. He couldn't tell for sure, but he thought if Wade were a sandwich, he'd be mostly baloney.

Wade rose from the chair, making it groan with relief. "Basically, you have to be willing to jump off a cliff for the woman you love. Figuratively speaking, of course. You don't really have to jump. But they like to think you're willing to. You know. . .sacrifice. That's the key."

"Sacrifice?" Zachary considered that word.

Wade hurled another chocolate in his mouth. "Owwee. Now these puppies are good."

"That's because they're Swiss. Dark chocolate with almond paste." Zachary tapped his finger on the desk.

"Guess I'd better have another one for the road." Wade took three more candies from the jar. "Got to keep up my strength."

Zachary frowned as he secured the lid on the candy jar.

"By the way, was this a dress-up day or something? Why are you wearing a Western shirt and a bolo?"

Zachary shook his head. "Don't ask."

"Oh, right. By the way, if this girl ever knew how smart you were, she'd fall into your arms. Brilliance equals good income potential, and that equals security for women. That's what they crave. Security and. . .well. . .romance."

"Is that what your wife said?"

"Yes." Wade rocked his head. "*After* we were married. A woman won't tell you her secrets until that gold band is snugly on her finger. And I—"

"But I thought you said sacrifice was the key to a woman's heart."

"Did I say that?" Wade laughed so hard he stretched his clothes beyond their limits, making his shirt snap open while simultaneously propelling a button across the room. He looked down at the empty buttonhole and chuckled again. "My wife has an endless supply of these little guys at home. See ya later."

After his coworker finally left, Zachary wrote on his palm: "Sacrifice, security, and romance." He figured that even as ridiculous as Wade could be, he may have hit on some honest answers to his dilemma. But what could he sacrifice for Nori, and how could he let her know she was secure with him? And what was romance, really? Flowers and poetry? Or was there more to it? Watching over terabytes of data was easy, but romance was not a known quantity.

Zachary flipped through the phone book and looked up the number of a local floral shop. He'd always liked lilies. They looked like trumpets about to announce something wonderful. Perhaps he'd send her a huge bouquet of them. *Wait a minute.* What was the flower his mother hated because the smell was so intense and awful? Surely it wasn't lilies. Maybe he had them confused with carnations or orchids.

With that last thought, the decision was settled in his mind—he would send lilies to Nori. He picked up the phone and, with renewed confidence, called the flower shop.

seven

The following day, Nori decided to skip lunch and head to the gym. Lizza was right. What would it hurt to tone up some of her softness? Besides, her gym membership had gone unused far too long.

Nori made her way into the large workout room, looking around in awe. A large crowd of men and women busied themselves, sweating on elliptical machines, trudging along on treadmills, and lifting weights. Not only had the place been overhauled, but so had the crowd. Since when had humans gotten thinner? And more angled? Where were all the rounder, gentler frames to make her feel at home? Maybe they were busy grazing at an all-you-can-eat pizza buffet. Sounded good, actually.

She let out a sigh but then raised her chin in resolve. Soon she would join them, but right now she had some shopping to do. After a quick visit to the sportswear shop at the front of the gym to select proper workout clothes, Nori slipped off to the changing room to put them on. She cocked her head at her reflection, studying the blue shorts and top and then giving herself an approving nod in the mirror. Hmm. She might not be a goddess, but she was far from a gargoyle. Maybe the workouts wouldn't be too painful or humiliating after all.

She headed back to the gym, ready to begin the toning and shaping. Where should she start? Ahh. There appeared to be a free elliptical machine, right next to a nice-looking guy who was busy flexing his muscles.

When Nori drew nearer to the stranger, she realized that it was the same guy from the bookstore. *Blake.* She wanted to walk the other way, but not wanting to give in to her nerves, she took her place on the machine.

Blake turned with a glance, his face lighting in a smile the minute he saw her. He brought his machine to a stop. "Hey, it's you."

Nori's face got tickly. "Yeah, it's me." She gave him an embarrassed nod and then tried to figure out how to get the machine to work. Apparently, she was smashing all the wrong buttons.

After a moment of watching her struggle, Blake leaned over and flipped a small switch.

"Thanks," she mouthed.

Within seconds they were both working out in unison.

"It's good to see you, Nori. I thought I'd never see you again."

"Really?" *This man named Blake cared about that fact?* Mind-boggling. Especially considering he was handsome enough to reduce even the most levelheaded woman to a helpless state of blather. But he sounded so heartfelt. "I'm glad to see you, too." In spite of herself, she giggled. *Oh brother, Nori. Don't get too excited.* Blake appeared to have such an eternally cheery temperament that he'd probably be ecstatic over a pile of clean socks.

Nori and Blake made light conversation while they worked out together. After a few minutes of exercise, though, Nori slowed her pace, hoping Blake wouldn't notice. A few times she felt out of breath, but in spite of her gasps and her already aching muscles, she was very pleased to discover they had two mutual friends through his church.

When they were finished, Blake cleared his throat. "As you may have heard, Grace Fellowship is having their annual spring festival and potluck dinner next week, and I was wondering if you'd like to go with me. Or maybe we could meet for coffee somewhere."

Nori blinked a few times, trying to find her voice again.

"Is there something in your eye?"

"I'm fine." Nori chuckled. The last thing Blake needed to see was her voracious appetite at a potluck dinner. "Coffee sounds. . .wonderful." She wanted to say unbelievable, but that would come off too pathetic.

Blake smiled again, showing his straight white teeth. "Well, how about I pick you up tomorrow evening at seven thirty, and we'll go to that coffee place on Central near Simon's Book Shoppe."

Nori nodded. "Sounds good. Very good. I'll give you my card when we're done."

"Good deal."

He followed her to the StairMaster and then to the stationary bikes. When she was worn out, Nori headed off to the changing room, promising to meet him up front with a business card in hand. She took a quick shower, slipped her work clothes back on, and practically sprinted to the front of the gym.

When Nori spotted Blake, she handed him her business card. "Here you are." Fortunately, she'd remembered to write her home phone number and address at the bottom.

"Thanks." He stared at the card. "So, you work at a candy shop?"

"I do. I own the place, in fact. Best candy in town."

"Not as sweet as the owner, I'll bet." He winked, smoothed his hair in a wall mirror, and then made his grand exit out the door, leaving her in a wake of designer cologne and some very welcome flattery.

Nori did her best not to holler, since others were looking

on, but she did do a quiet little jig around the room and chanted to herself, "Yes, yes, yes." She knew she looked silly, but she didn't care. She had a date. A real one. One she could brag about to Lizza. One she could dream about on a cold evening when no one was around to offer her cocoa. And a date she could remind herself of when she felt like a frump.

The word *frump* seeped into her pile of worries. She thought of all the improvements Lizza had suggested. *Sometime soon, I think I'll get a makeover at the mall.* With renewed resolve, Nori straightened her shoulders and strode toward the door.

She made the drive back to work with an irrepressible grin. Candy never looked so good, and the rest of the day at Sweet Nothings floated by on a cloud of blissful expectation.

❧

After opening the door to her apartment, she kicked off her shoes and wiggled her toes. For some reason, her feet no longer ached. Ahh. Dates worked like endorphins.

Just as she was about to fix dinner, the doorbell rang. She walked to the door and looked through the peephole. Nori saw a young woman with a giant bouquet of lilies. She opened the door. "Hi."

"Are you Nori Kelly?"

"That's me."

"Then these beauties are for you."

"I can't believe it."

"Well, enjoy." The young woman's nose twitched a bit as she handed Nori the vase of lilies.

"Oh, I will. Thank you." She gave the woman a generous tip. "They're so beautiful." But the second the door went shut, Nori sneezed. Five times. *Oh no.* And what was that pungent odor? Something smelled like smoldering garbage. The lilies.

She held her breath as she poked around the bouquet for a

card. Hmm. Nothing. Whoever had sent them was sweet, but the smell was unbearable, so she placed the urn of flowers on an end table in the corner.

Then Nori sat down on the other side of the room, sighing and staring at the bouquet. In spite of the bizarre fragrance, the flowers were exquisite, and she certainly didn't want to be caught complaining since they were the first flowers any man had ever given her.

Blake must have sent them. Perhaps it was a new custom to butter up a woman before he took her out. She hadn't dated in so long, men might be sending gifts of shrubbery and small goats for all she knew. But then she wondered how Blake could have known she'd say yes to his invitation to coffee. She thought he must be a very confident guy. Or at least a guy who wasn't used to hearing the word *no*.

❧

Zachary paced his apartment, a nervous wreck. Through a crack in the door, he'd watched the delivery take place. Lilies had been the perfect choice, at least from his vantage point. Not too personal. Not too intense. Just right for a girl like Nori.

Surely she would have to agree.

He rubbed his hands together, energized. He'd done it. He'd actually sent flowers to a woman. Soon he would work up the courage to let her know he was the one who'd sent the lilies. Then, about the time she opened her mouth to thank him, he would ask her out on a date.

eight

The next day at Sweet Nothings, Nori just stood back and watched as Lizza told all of the regular customers about the big date with Blake. In fact, Lizza was delighted to repeat the story loudly over and over to Harvey, who was a little hard of hearing. Evelyn, another customer, got so excited she celebrated Nori's good fortune by buying chocolate truffles for everyone in the store.

When Lizza had them frothed up, they started pelting Nori with advice like rice at a wedding. A middle-aged woman who frequented the shop said, "When you're out on your date, act unassuming. But don't be *too* inconspicuous. Just a down-to-earth kind of shyness. That's how I got my husband."

"Who said anything about a husband?" Nori asked.

Another woman waved off the suggestion. "No, no. You've got to be bold these days. And offer to pick up the check. That's how it's done if you want to stay in the game."

"Game?" Nori flinched. "But—"

"You *do* want to get married someday, don't you?"

"Yes, but. . ." How could she share her heart in front of a roomful of people she barely knew? Of course she had longings to marry, to have a family. But talking about the date openly would only make the sting more severe if something went wrong.

Another young woman, recently heartbroken, listened in with a somber look on her face as she ordered a pound of chocolates. "What's the point?" she asked. "They're just going to break your heart anyway." With a sigh, she ordered an extra half pound—for the road.

In spite of the wildly assorted responses, Nori could hardly contain her excitement. It seemed like every few minutes, something—or someone—reminded her of that fact. She was going on a date with Blake, and she felt like a windup toy on its last turn, ready to whirl. And what a wonderful specimen Blake was. He seemed to embody almost everything she could hope for in a man.

Around noon, Zachary Martin arrived at the shop. Today, he appeared to be dressed in more normal attire. Well, normal for him. He still looked a bit on the geeky side, but his smile warmed her heart. Then again, everything seemed to warm her heart today.

Zachary surprised her with more conversation than usual. In fact, he started with something quite flattering. "You look nice today." Zachary's eyes sparkled with anticipation.

She glanced down at her apron, covered in powdered sugar. "Mmm. . .thanks."

"That's a really nice *floral* print." He pointed to her blouse.

Nori shrugged and thanked him, but she couldn't figure out why he would notice such an ordinary and rather faded blouse. She tried to turn her attention to other customers, but Zachary kept appearing at her side, asking questions, commenting on the decor of the shop, especially the flowers on the tables. What was up with this guy?

After the crowd thinned, Lizza approached with a gleam in her eye. "I have the perfect idea."

"What's that?"

"You need a shopping spree—to get ready for your big date."

"Oh no, I can't. I'm working. Besides"—Nori lowered her voice so that the customers couldn't hear—"we're just going out for coffee. It's not that big of a deal."

"Are you kidding? You should take full advantage of this.

Go to the mall. Get a makeover." Lizza raised her hands like she was directing an orchestra. "Seize the moment!"

Nori rolled her eyes, trying not to get too worked up. What if Blake's real plan was to ask her to join a multilevel marketing venture, or something crazy like that? "Maybe he just needs a chubby friend who looks sympathetic," she said to Lizza. "One who looks like she has extra softness to help her friends absorb the blows of life. You know, like those yellow bumper guards on the freeway."

Lizza erupted in laughter. "You're hysterical. Do you know that? But you gotta stop putting yourself down."

As Nori shrugged, she couldn't help but notice Zachary's penetrating gaze. Was he listening in on their conversation?

"This is going to be the best date of your life," Lizza announced in a voice far too loud. "So get out of here. Go shopping."

Nori shook her head, grinning, and then pulled off her apron. Yes, she would go to the mall. For Blake Lawrence, she might even go to the moon.

❧

After Nori left out the front door in a whirl of happiness, Zachary slumped down onto a chair in the shop. He slid another chocolate-covered coffee bean between his lips. He no longer nonchalantly tossed candy into his mouth, since he was apparently a wimpy kind of guy who easily choked on candy.

He moaned to himself. How could things have gone so wrong? Not only had Nori *not* taken his bait about the lilies, she apparently already had a date with another guy. Someone named Blake.

That name sounded like an iron kind of dude who heaved timbers with one arm behind his back and wrestled Brahma bulls just for fun. Zachary was certain he wasn't a guy who choked on girly mints. He could picture Blake now—tall, bronzed, with fitness-center biceps. The kind of man who made most women lose all their good sense.

After sitting for a moment or two longer, he quietly slipped out of his seat and made his way to the door. The jingling of the bell was the only indicator he'd moved on. But move on he must. If Nori had her sights set on someone else, it would be wrong to ask her out now. Wouldn't it?

As he walked back toward his office, Zachary spent some time in prayer. He gave the situation to the Lord, realizing how wrong it would be to pursue a relationship with Nori if the Lord hadn't ordained it.

By the time he reached the office, Zachary's heart was broken in two. How was it possible to lose something you'd never won in the first place?

With a deep sigh, he dropped into his chair, ready to push that question—and all thoughts of women—out of his mind.

nine

After slipping into a blue linen dress and giving herself yet another touch-up with her new makeup, Nori felt ready to share some serious caffeine with Blake Lawrence. At least she wouldn't embarrass him. She glanced in the hall mirror again. Not bad. The sapphire colors in the dress enhanced her hair and skin tones rather than washing her out, and her eye shadow, lipstick, and blush were actually in the right places—this time she hadn't colored outside the lines.

Dressed and more than ready for her date, Nori waited for Blake by the door. Twenty minutes later, she started fiddling with her purse—opening and shutting the clasp, checking her lipstick, popping a breath mint, and generally wilting like a pile of tissues left in the rain.

Maybe the invitation is a hoax. Maybe one of his friends had talked him into asking her out as a joke. But Blake's face had been so kind. He didn't look like a guy who would fail to show up for a date unless something terrible happened—like broken limbs or a plane crash or maybe an abscessed tooth.

Nori watched the second hand on the big clock on the end table. With each stroke, she felt as if her life was pouring out of her. She had no idea where her spirit was going, but she felt drained and suddenly old. A single tear rolled down Nori's cheek. She wiped the wetness away and rose from her chair to change her clothes.

Just as Nori made it to the bedroom, she heard the doorbell ring. Hoping Blake had finally come, she swung open the door and let it bang against the wall, which confirmed the

47

fact that she was feeling a little too eager and way too upset.

Blake raked his fingers through his hair. "I'm really sorry for being late."

Nori nodded. "Sure." She knew he must have gotten held up with something dreadfully important. "Is everything okay?"

"You'll never believe this." He tugged on his hair. "I was in the middle of a haircut, and this girl starts tossing and whacking my hair like she's making a salad."

Should I laugh or weep or console? Nori compromised with a grin.

Blake seemed satisfied. "I had to find another salon and get a *real* haircut. So. . .I mean. . .what do you think? Do I look ridiculous?"

Nori swatted at the butterfly of sarcasm that flitted through her head. She chewed on her lower lip to think of a *real* reply. *Was I almost stood up because of hair?* She found her vocal cords. "You look great. Would you like to come in for a minute?"

Blake relaxed into a smirk and ambled through the door. "Sometimes I have highlights done, but I thought I could get by this time."

"Oh?" She'd naively guessed his highlights were natural from being outdoors. Nori didn't want to imagine Blake sitting in the salon chair with tinfoil spikes coming out of his head. She winced, trying to shake the vision from her mind.

They sat down across from each other. For a moment neither one of them said anything, so Nori did a casual inspection of his attire. She had to admit Blake radiated splendor like the sun in his designer denims and tangerine shirt. In fact, she knew few men who could pull off that color with such panache.

"So, what are your thoughts?" Blake suddenly asked.

"My thoughts? Uhh. . ." Nori panicked, thinking she'd missed something.

"You know, should I have gotten the highlights this time?"

Blake puckered his brow. "What do you really think?"

She sighed. *I think quantum physics is looking good.* "You made a wise decision to wait," she finally got herself to say. "No sense in overbleaching. It will ruin your hair." Her words just sort of evaporated along with her hopes of a promising evening.

Blake nodded as if she'd said something profound.

After more conversation about hair and grooming products and salons, they headed out to the coffee shop. A few minutes later, they were seated at a cozy table with two cups of steaming coffees.

Nori inhaled the aroma of homemade pastries and fresh coffee as she admired the homey room—tables trimmed in gingham and vases filled with roses. What an ideal place for a first date. She took a sip of her cinnamon latte.

Glancing around, she also noticed that women were staring at Blake. And not just a fleeting look or two. They gawked with big dreamy eyes like they were groupies and he was their rock star. She wondered what that felt like to be born so pretty that everyone couldn't stop looking and admiring. Perhaps people thought if they were close enough to someone beautiful, they would somehow be more beautiful. A validation thing. *Is that what I'm doing?*

Maybe she could still salvage the date with a change of subject. "So what do you do for a living?"

"Oh, I do all kinds of odd jobs. I've been a waiter and a tour guide and a salesman. I also do some modeling. It pays really well when I can get the gigs."

Nori took another slow slurp from her cup.

"But I feel kinda guilty getting all that money for just standing around." Blake fingered his cup. "By the way, I've been thinking about the name of your candy shop, Sweet Nothings." He raised a provocative brow. "What does it mean?"

Nori felt her face heat up a little. "Well, sweet nothings are. . .you know, the things lovers whisper to each other. You've never heard that saying before?"

"Yeah, I have. I just wanted to hear what you'd say." Then Blake laughed. One of those big horsey laughs straight out of a cartoon.

Nori took in a deep breath, trying to focus on reality and get her eye to stop twitching. Then she took a paper napkin and dabbed at the perspiration on her forehead.

"Are you okay?" He gave her a curious stare. " 'Cause sometimes you look like you're in pain."

"I'm fine. Really."

Blake grinned. "Good deal."

Nori thought she might as well ask the ultimate question. "I was just curious. . . . I always love to know what a person's favorite candy is."

Blake picked up a saltshaker and rolled it around in his hand. "Mmm. Heavy question." He shook his finger. "Oh, I get it. You're trying to figure out what kind of guy I am from the candy I eat. Right?"

"Yeah." She guessed he'd buy some kind of gelatinous candy. Maybe something in the family of gooey animal-shaped treats.

Blake brightened. "Well, I like those little gummy candies that are in different shapes and colors."

Nori almost choked on her latte.

"You okay?"

She nodded.

"The blue and white sharks are my favorite." His brawny shoulders went up in a shrug; then he puckered his brow. "I'll bet that sounds pretty stupid."

Nori decided to take the high road. "Well, it can make you come off like you're not afraid to be childlike. You're man enough to be whimsical, and—"

"Yeah, that's it." He pointed in the air. "That word you just said. That's what I am."

"Uh-huh." Nori took an extended swig of her brew as her gaze drifted over to the second hand on the wall clock, which appeared to be moving with agonizing slowness. *And they say time doesn't stand still.*

Blake took a tentative sip of his vanilla cappuccino. "Owee, that's still pretty hot." He pointed to his lips. "Gotta be careful not to burn these babies. One time, I nicked up my chin helping my mom with some yard work, and I lost a modeling gig." He moved his cup out of the way and leaned toward her. "So, missy, what do you think is the best candy of all time? I mean, you can choose the best. Right?"

Nori straightened up and took in a deep breath. With some effort, maybe she could give the evening one more try. "Well, I do have one favorite candy that is quite exceptional and rather pricey. It's—"

"You know, most of the girls I've dated are way too skinny and kinda blank. But you're different."

"Blank?"

Blake reached over to Nori and moved a strand of hair from her cheek. "You're smart. I mean, you'd have to be pretty intelligent to own a business."

"Thanks." Nori powered up for a smile. She wanted to say, "Yeah, us chubbies have all that extra fat to fuel our brains," but instead she replied, "By the way, thank you for the flowers."

Blake leaned in. "Now this is a time for you to see what an honest guy I am."

"Why is that?"

"Well, it sure would be easy for me to take credit, but. . .I can't." Blake grinned.

"Really?" Nori tapped her fingers on her cup. "So, you

didn't have lilies delivered to my apartment?"

"No." Blake laughed. "I would *never* send lilies to a woman. They stink."

❧

The rest of the evening didn't improve. In fact, Nori found herself glancing around and squelching a yawn.

She liked Blake. He was a kind man but also a simple man, and perhaps a bit too self-absorbed. Nori thought she must be out of her mind for such thoughts, since she had no right to be choosy. At all. And Blake was as handsome as any man could get. And yet, no matter how hard she tried, she couldn't force an attraction anymore than she could change the direction of the wind.

Later, after what seemed like a long journey home, Blake stood at Nori's front door. He leaned on the door frame and gave her a heavy-lidded look like she'd seen in the movies. Dead giveaway. He was going to give her a good night kiss. What should she do?

"I'm not sure if I mentioned it before, but I think you look nice this evening. Very nice," Blake added, his voice going down a couple of octaves.

"Thank you." Nori reached in her purse for her keys. "And thanks for the coffee. It was good."

"Yes, it was. It was all so good." Then Blake went quiet.

Nori held her breath, wondering if a kiss might put a better glow on the evening. Perhaps Blake just wanted to say thank-you for her pleasant company. Or maybe he would just kiss her on the forehead like a small child.

The waiting and pondering was over the moment Blake leaned down and placed his lips over hers.

Nori closed her eyes, praying her first real kiss would be apart from all other sensations and feelings. Would it send her flying off into space? Indeed, the kiss was warm and not altogether unpleasant, but something was missing. In fact, as the kiss intensified, the stirrings became. . .what? Comical? Instead of soaring into space, she rose only a few feet off the ground—in a toy rocket. The plastic kind that fizzles and plummets to the earth. *Cut it out, Nori. This is difficult enough.*

They both pulled away at the same time and then stared at each other. Another awkward moment came hovering over them. Then, at the same instant, they both burst out laughing.

"Tell me what you're thinking." Blake touched her sleeve.

Nori covered her mouth. "I can't."

"Yes, you can. I think we're both thinking the same thing."

She circled her hands around her middle. "But it might hurt your feelings."

"You mean worse than when you laughed after our kiss." Blake chuckled.

"But you laughed, too. . .even harder." Nori's face heated in embarrassment. "But I'm sorry if it hurt your feelings. I really—"

"Come on, you're stalling. Just say what you want to say. I'll try to be man enough to take it."

Nori touched Blake's arm. "It's like. . .well. . .like we're just friends or family."

"I noticed it, too. But I think it's a good thing. You see, I'm an only child, and I've always needed a sibling." Blake covered her hand with his and knelt down. "Nori Kelly, would you be my sister?"

Nori laughed. "I would be happy to be your sister."

After they chatted for a moment or two longer and he'd given her a brotherly hug, they parted for the evening.

Before Nori shut the door, she saw someone back away into the shadows. Someone had seen Blake kissing her. And that someone looked like Zachary. Likely, he was walking to his apartment from the other direction, saw them, and didn't want to interrupt a private moment. Or maybe they'd embarrassed Zachary, and he'd taken off. Regardless, the whole thing felt awkward, especially in light of the way the date had turned out.

Nori locked the dead bolt and sank into a chair. "Well, I'm still princess of the friendship date." She looked upward past the ceiling. *Lord, why do I have such an intense desire to marry and have a family? If You put this need in me, then please fulfill it or give me the patience to wait for it. But if this dream would cause me a grief I cannot comprehend, then please take this desire away. I'm getting so weary of it.*

And then revelation came to Nori—Zachary had sent the flowers. It all made sense now. He had been trying to drop hints at the candy shop—all those references to the floral print in her blouse and the flowers on the tables.

Hmm. Zachary Martin. Maybe, in spite of his clumsy efforts, Zachary was really trying to romance her. But why? He'd never even asked her out. Mysteries were abundant, and they all seemed to be taking up residence in her ordinary life.

❧

Zachary slumped on his couch—a couch which sat next to Nori's wall. He knew he was torturing himself, sitting there with the hope of being nearer to her, but he felt like a good wallow in misery was in order.

The facts felt devastating, since he'd witnessed Nori kissing another man. Must be that Blake fellow. And sadly, he was as good-looking as Zachary had predicted him to be. He wondered how long they'd been dating. Were they in love? Were all Zachary's chances to win Nori gone?

He looked at the receipt for the flowers and crumpled it. To say he felt letdown was such an understatement. He was so disappointed, in fact, that he tossed his copy of *Courtship for Idiots* out the window. Well, not exactly out of the window.

That would be littering. He stuck the book behind the curtain, hoping it would gather dust and eventually disintegrate into subatomic particles.

And yet, he couldn't blame anyone or anything. What claim did he have on Nori? None at all. And hadn't he prayed about all of this, giving it over to the Lord?

Maybe what he needed was time to get his thoughts together, to come up with another workable plan. Tomorrow morning he would do just that.

ten

The next morning in the clear light of a new day, Zachary decided his "workable plans" hadn't been too impressive or effective. Maybe what he'd been missing was some fresh air and a chat with God.

He snatched up his car keys and drove to one of his favorite hiking places. After parking his car and zipping up his jacket, he started the mile-long walk to the Mountain Tower. Zachary saw no tourists, so he prayed out loud as he hiked up the paved road.

"Lord, maybe I'm getting ahead of You, trying to force a relationship with Nori that's outside Your leading. You know how much I love her, and yet I know any relationship outside of Your will would only be a distraction."

Regrettably, in spite of his best intentions, Zachary found himself sidetracked rather quickly. His thoughts kept shifting to Nori's date. No matter how Blake appeared on the outside, he didn't really think he was Nori's type. And that ridiculous laugh of his. How could Nori stand it?

He slowed his pace and reality hit. "Why am I always trying to manipulate what I can't control? It's like I'm always trying to convince God what's best." Zachary surrendered himself to the peaceful solitude of the moment and to what God might have to say to him. *Yes, to get ahead of God would only complicate things.* If there was to be a relationship with Nori, it would have to be in the Lord's timing.

He picked up a rock and studied it. *Sandstone. Pretty typical for the Ouachita Mountains.* Probably from an ancient beach or river. He pressed the stone inside his hand, letting his palm and fingers mold around its solid mass.

His thoughts turned to the recent hours he'd spent in the Word of God, thumbing through the pages, looking for the Lord's take on love. "That's the kind of love I want," he said, "one rooted in faith." And so, as he walked, he committed himself once again to a deeper relationship with the Lord.

As Zachary continued hiking up the hill, he realized that even though the spiritual side was the most important part of his life, he also had a few things he could work on in the natural. Maybe it was time to focus a little more on his appearance. He'd gotten sloppy over the past few years. In fact, he'd almost given up on himself. But no more. Some simple changes along with a little discipline would put the wheels in motion. Wasn't that how he handled things at work, after all?

He finished his hike and looked up at the tower, which promised an amazing view of the town as well as the woods and lakes and hills he'd grown to love. Suddenly, a squirrel caught his attention as it scampered up high in a tree. The branches above him had already budded out, which lit the woods with a pale green luster. A cardinal, stark against the blooming dogwood, rested for a moment and then fluttered away, deep into the forest.

Zachary breathed in. The crisp breeze gave courage to his plan. "First, I will lay low and give Nori some space." Peace settled around him as he spoke. "Secondly, while I'm busy lying low, I'll make some necessary enhancements without making myself into a fool. If and when the time comes. . . Nori deserves the very best."

❧

As the days passed, Zachary was good to his word. He dealt with the basics. He got a new haircut—nothing spiky or too trendy. He made a habit of wearing only pressed shirts and pants without white socks, and he was fitted for some contact lenses. The red indentations on his nose, which were made from wearing his glasses, began to fade. At times he barely recognized himself.

Next, he decided he should expand his mind. He should go to Simon's Book Shoppe and buy something inspiring or literary or romantic. Or all of the above. He would be able to understand Nori better if he could get inside the head of a woman.

One evening after dinner, Zachary locked up and made his way down the hallway to the elevator. He heard Nori coming out of her apartment and turned back to her. "Hello."

"Hi." She smiled at him.

A nice smile. Not the usual obligatory grin, but an expression that appeared genuine and inviting. Should he make a move now? No. He wouldn't get ahead of God. He would wait. Zachary reminded himself that "lying low" were his watchwords. *But she's never smiled at me like that before. Ever.* Yes, he should do it now. Or maybe not. He stood in front of the elevator in a fit of indecision. He waited for Nori to catch up to him before he pushed the button. "Uh, Nori?"

"Yes?"

Oh brother. Now he was committed to talking. Should he thank her again for saving his life? "I'm going to Simon's Book Shoppe."

"You are? Sounds good. I like that store."

Nori certainly is friendly. That was new. Maybe now *was* the time. "You want to come along?"

"I'd like to, but I've got this meeting to attend. It's with some of the small-business owners." Nori licked her lips. "But maybe another time. Okay?"

He nodded. "Absolutely."

The elevator doors opened, and they rode down together.

Zachary stood next to Nori, basking in the glow of her sweet smile.

Moments later, at Simon's Book Shoppe, Zachary stood perusing shelves and shelves of novels. He picked out a historical romance, paid for it, and then settled himself in one of the cushy chairs.

Soft classical music ebbed and flowed around him, providing a pleasant ambience for reading his book. As he looked over the dedication, which was a tribute of devotion from the author to his beloved wife, Zachary recalled something from Proverbs he'd recently read: *"Let love and faithfulness never leave you; bind them around your neck, write them on the tablet of your heart."* Had he been loving and faithful in all things, not just in his feelings for Nori? He wasn't sure, but he hoped so.

Thoughts of Nori made him think of Song of Solomon. A brief passage came to mind. . . . *"Your hair is like royal tapestry; the king is held captive by its tresses. How beautiful you are and how pleasing, O love, with your delights!"* Ah yes. Nori was indeed delightful in every way. He sighed as he stared at the book title in front of him, *Fields of Amber Light.* He read the opening lines:

> *I always knew I would love her. She had a smile one could never forget: soft, welcoming, transcendent. She was the winsome creature of my childhood, and now to know her love in return was unfathomable joy. I know, as I have always known, that our love will warm the earth. It will sustain the stars. It will summon the songs of angels.*

The words moved him, making him wish he could be creative and expressive. Perhaps that was what poetry and novels were for—to articulate the feelings of a common man like himself. He pondered the words "winsome creature" and "unfathomable joy" and thought the author did very well in mirroring the fervent prose of the love verses in the Bible. *Beautiful.*

Zachary heard someone walking toward him, so he glanced up.

Nori stood in front of him wearing a pale green dress and a smile that rivaled the sun.

"You changed your mind?" he heard himself murmur.

She crossed her arms. "I decided I didn't want to waste my life sitting in meetings."

Zachary tried to keep his cool as Nori sat down next to him. "You look different. In a good kind of way."

"Thanks." Nori folded her hands in her lap, looking suddenly shy.

"And you have makeup on." He tried to enjoy her beauty without gaping.

"I just hope I didn't go overboard with the blush and lip gloss."

"You're absolutely radiant. . .like Sirius." *Oh boy. Talk about going overboard.* He meant the praise, but he knew men just didn't blurt out things like that.

She leaned her elbow on the chair and looked at him. "And what is Sirius?"

"The brightest star in the sky."

Nori looked down at her hands. "Thank you, Zachary. I think that's the finest compliment anyone has ever given me."

"You're welcome." He thought their banter was going better than expected. He couldn't help but wonder about Blake. Perhaps her date with him hadn't worked out.

She looked down at his book. "What are you reading?"

He held up the novel. "*Fields of Amber Light.*"

"What kind of book is it?"

Zachary cleared his throat. "It's sort of a historical literary. . . romance."

"I haven't read that many romance novels."

"Really?" Zachary set the book down on the arm of the chair. "But I thought women read them all the time."

Nori looked at the cover again. "It looks fascinating."

"Well, this is my first." Zachary felt his underarms start to sweat. "Do you want to hear some of it?"

She nodded. "I do."

"Okay." Zachary almost forgot where he was. In fact, as he got caught up in the romantic moment and gazed into her eyes, he almost forgot *who* he was.

He gathered his senses and opened the novel somewhere close to the front. He cleared his throat and began reading:

"We first met in a field of clover, found by the sun and lit with gold. She and I escaped our dins of clamor to partake of those amber lights. Bees took to the air while we laughed about all things that gave us delight and all things that made us humble. When the amber lights had faded and the bees had made their honey, we returned to our worlds, lost in heart but found in love."

Zachary looked at Nori.

Nori clasped her hands over her heart. "That was delightful to hear out loud."

"Yes, it was." Zachary realized his eyes had filled with mist. His face went hot as he sniffled a bit. To Nori's credit, she didn't laugh at him. "Some of the fantasy novels I've read are written in this literary technique. A poetic style sort of gets to the heart of things in a roundabout way, and then when you least expect it, the meaning sort of steals your heart." *Did I actually say that? Am I still alive and breathing? Thank You, God.*

"That's true. And beautifully said." Nori shook her head. "I've been so busy running my business, I haven't taken enough time to read. I've missed a lot. And I'm embarrassed to say, I've even skipped my devotion time with the Lord." She sighed. "Well, my excuses are weak, but my determination in returning to it is sincere."

Zachary felt fresh out of words. He panicked a bit.

"So, you said you read fantasy novels?"

"I read science fiction and computer manuals." Well, that came off as exciting as a disposal full of sludge.

Nori touched Zachary's arm. "By the way, thank you for the flowers. They were. . .well, *pretty* to look at."

He looked at Nori's hand, the one that still touched his arm. Zachary hoped she wouldn't notice his erratic breathing. "Uhh. . .you're welcome." Things were going so well between them, he thought maybe he was dreaming. "But I'll bet you like roses better."

She pulled away. "Why do you say that?"

"I don't know. I think because you have so many pictures of roses all around your candy store."

"Oh, you noticed. I do like roses. Especially bridal pink."

"Trust me. I *will* remember that."

Nori raised an eyebrow. "I'm sure you will."

She's flirting with me. Zachary leaned forward in his chair, now feeling euphoric. What were the chances of Nori sitting with him tonight, talking about her favorite kind of roses? It all seemed impossible.

Nori's cell phone came to life. She looked at the caller and then at him. "It's my mother. I'd better get it."

Zachary nodded for her to take the call.

❧

Nori wondered what could be wrong. *Mom rarely calls me.* "Hi. What a surprise. How are you?" She remained silent, absorbing her mother's news, which became graver by the second. "But I don't understand. Why would either of you do something like that?" She clutched at her heart. "Why can't we talk about this now? Okay. All right." Nori tried to calm her breathing. "I'll call you later tonight." She closed her phone and let out a long puff of air.

"What is it?" Zachary asked.

"My parents." Nori's arms went limp as her eyes filled with tears. "They're getting a divorce."

eleven

"My mom and dad. . .they had a good marriage." Nori latched onto the armchair and squeezed until her fingers ached. "In fact, they'd gone to Paris to celebrate another wedding anniversary. They just got home." She felt her stomach go woozy. *Stay calm. You're not going to throw up in a bookstore.*

Zachary shook his head. "I'm so sorry."

Nori nodded and then plummeted back into her fears. Her parents had always loved each other. Hadn't they? "I don't understand. I thought they were having a wonderful vacation." Tears ran down her cheek. "What could have gone wrong?" She wasn't used to showing so much emotion in public, but somehow decorum didn't matter to her right now.

Zachary reached out to her.

Nori noticed his hands shaking. *Why would he be so affected?*

"I wish I could do something for you." Zachary blushed and pulled away.

"I do, too." Nori rested her head in her hands. How could this be? Even when most of the people around her were cutting themselves into bits on the sharp edges of divorce, she had always consoled herself with the idea that one couple would always remain steady. One couple, by the grace of God, would stay intact—her parents. "My mother and father didn't have the perfect marriage, but I'd held them up as an example of real commitment. I'd put my trust in them." Nori turned to him. "When so many good marriages in America die, what hope do people have in love?"

Zachary looked stunned with the question. "I think there's still hope. There's *always* hope."

Nori stared at her hands, which were now trembling. "Are your parents still married?"

He lowered his gaze. "No."

Something inside of Nori shifted—something that moved her toward a helpless anguish. More tears came. They were real, and they weren't going away anytime soon. She dabbed the wetness away with the sleeve of her dress. Several book browsers drifted by, but she didn't care who saw her.

Zachary pulled a handkerchief out of his pocket and handed it to her. "Do you want to go over to the coffee shop? We could talk about it." He leaned toward her, worry covering his face.

Nori blew her nose. "No, but thanks. I'm not sure talking will do any good. My mom sounded determined."

"Maybe you could discuss this with your parents," Zachary said. "And pray they change their minds."

"I *will* pray, but my parents have this thing called free will." Nori shook her head. "I really need time to think. Time alone." She rose from her chair and picked up her purse. "I'm going home."

Zachary stood up next to her. "You shouldn't drive when you're this upset. It isn't safe. Why don't you—"

"I'll be fine. Well, at least my drive will be."

Zachary stuffed his hands into his pockets, looking bewildered.

"Well, then"—Nori touched his sleeve—"good-bye." She looked at him one more time and then walked out into the night.

She drove home as the shock of her mother's news seeped deeply into her spirit like a slow-acting poison. How could something like that happen? Was no marriage secure? Did love and commitment mean nothing anymore?

Nori shut her apartment door and trudged into the kitchen, her feet feeling as though they were dragging ten-pound weights. She took the tinfoil off a deep-dish cherry pie and dug into it with a big serving spoon. The bite was gooey sweet, but it did nothing to ease her pain.

Even when her life had been fraught with loneliness, she'd always managed by keeping herself busy with work. But this? Now another piece of her life was whirling out of control. She could always petition the Almighty, but even He couldn't force her parents to stop the divorce proceedings.

She clutched at her dress, twisting the material into knots and feeling abandoned and scared. Did her parents have a terrible fight? Had they fallen out of love? Maybe one of them was having a midlife crisis or an affair. Her endless questions brought no answers.

Nori felt the walls of her sanctuary, solid and sure, collapse around her. Even as a little girl she'd always gathered her dolls together for weddings, all in the hopes of recreating the marital joy she thought she'd seen in her parents' eyes. Had she imagined their love for each other? Or had they only been pretending?

She dug into the pie again with her spoon and brought another large chunk of the pastry to her mouth. *What does it matter if I try to lose weight to catch the attention of the opposite sex?* Nori shoveled a few more bites of cherry pie in her mouth until her cheeks were packed with pastry. Cherry juice dribbled down her chin. She wiped it off on the sleeve of her dress.

Disgusted with herself, she dropped the spoon on the table, promising herself to get in shape for her own health and benefit. Nothing more. She shoved the pie to the other side of the table but pushed too hard. The pie dish landed on the ceramic tile floor, crashing and making a crimson splatter of glass and berries.

She just stared at the mess. Soon tears gave way to heaving sobs as she lowered her head to the kitchen table. *What I'd always feared is true—love really isn't enough. Please, God, You are more than welcome to jump in here and intervene. Anytime, Lord. I know You're here with me. I have believed that ever since I came to know You when I was a girl. But right now, I don't feel Your presence. I feel frantic with all this news. Please, Lord, take these troubles away. I don't think I can handle them.*

Finally, when her tears slowed and her despair eased a bit, Nori raised her head from the table. She glanced at a greeting card she'd stuck on her fridge. A frog with bulbous eyes stared at her from the front of the card. The comical amphibian was Lizza's reminder that she might have to kiss a pond full of frogs to find her prince. She released a gloomy chuckle. "Well, Lizza, I'm no longer interested in frogs or princes."

Nori picked up the phone and tried calling her parents, but no one answered. Just as she pushed in the numbers again, a knock interrupted her. She dragged herself to the front door but wasn't sure if she'd answer it.

Zachary stood on the other side of the door with a lost puppy expression that would normally make her feel guilty. But now she felt nothing. She stood there, waiting for him to go, but he didn't move. *Maybe I should at least open the door.* He was no longer a prospective date, but he was still a fellow human being.

Nori decided not to check her eyes, even though she thought they must be red and bloated and festooned with black rings of mascara. Didn't matter to her, so she just opened the door.

"Hi." Zachary had a casual pose, but he appeared uneasy. "What's up?"

A look of pain crossed his face. "You know, when my parents told me they were getting a divorce, I got pretty messed up," he said. "I held everything in, and that was pretty dangerous. I was like this walking time bomb ready to detonate at any moment." His eyes got big, and his fingers contorted into claws.

Nori was on the verge of a smile but wasn't about to give in so easily. "I know you want to come in and listen to my story and then give me advice. I appreciate that. I really do. But I don't know the story. They won't tell me any details. I think they're afraid I'll try to talk them out of it."

Zachary lowered his gaze as if he was praying, and then he looked up with more confidence. "I have this thing I do."

Nori groaned inside. *What can he mean now?* She just wanted to go lie down and sleep for maybe a month or two. "What is it?"

"Well, I have this ritual. . .for when I get upset about something. Or I'm disappointed. I have these ingredients that come together to make a pretty impressive cup of cocoa. I know it's maybe a little simplistic. But there's something about cocoa. . .that's settling. If you come over, I'll make you some."

Nori swallowed, her throat making a funny squeaking sound. How could he have known that cocoa was her favorite beverage of all time? Good for comfort, reflection, and camaraderie. But as always, Zachary's timing could not have been more haywire. "I don't know. . ."

"You won't regret it. And I promise I won't pressure you to talk about. . .you know. Anyway, I'll let you just drink the cocoa in peace and go home."

Oh well, what did she have to lose? Her only plans were to cry her heart out until she fell asleep from exhaustion. Homemade cocoa sounded like at least a temporary reprieve. "Maybe just for a few minutes."

Zachary's face lit up.

She already regretted her decision. "I should clean up my face."

"You don't need to. You look beautiful."

Oh come on. Nori wanted to roll her eyes but didn't. But she ignored the cleanup after all and followed Zachary to his apartment.

Ivan Wentworth, a bachelor she'd been curious about for months, locked up his apartment and strode toward them. "Hello."

Nori didn't turn away, even though she knew she looked like something approaching ghastly. "Hi."

Ivan stared at Nori for a moment as he passed by, his face flashing with horror as if he'd seen the headless horseman. Then Ivan hurried down the hallway.

In regular times, such an incident would have bothered Nori. First of all because of her hideous appearance, but secondly, because everyone on the floor of their apartment, especially the gossips, would soon say that she and Zachary were dating. And that they'd been arguing, since her eyes were all puffy and red. But why should she care? Why would it matter now? She had no interest in Ivan or Zachary or anyone.

Nori walked through Zachary's living room and looked around. Impressive. He didn't have a lot of decorating skills, but she was startled at all the expensive furnishings. Maybe Lizza had been right—perhaps geeks *did* rule the world. "You have a nice apartment."

"Thank you." Zachary blushed at her compliment. "Why don't we go into the kitchen? That is, you know, if you want to. Would you like to?"

Come on, Zachary, don't start up with the nervous routine again. It's a waste of your valuable time. I'm not going to marry you, so let's just settle down and maybe we can be friends. "Sure. The kitchen sounds fine."

"The kitchen is the best part of any abode."

"What do you mean?" Nori wasn't sure if she was up to hearing all his comments on kitchens.

"I guess when I was growing up, anything good that was happening was always in the kitchen. You know, baking, eating, talking. . .science projects." Zachary smiled at Nori as he led her into the kitchen. "You can have a seat right here while I make your cocoa." He pulled out a chair for her as if he were a nobleman and she were his lady.

Nori sat down and waited. She glanced around his kitchen. It looked somewhat empty, and yet there were personal touches here and there. Things that didn't look at all that kitchen-y but items that must have meant something to him—a framed poster of some of the characters from the original *Star Trek* shows, shelves and shelves of books, an old-fashioned telephone dismantled and set out in pieces on the counter, and to her surprise, a notable array of copper pots and pans. Even a cast-iron skillet.

"So how do you make your cocoa?" She hoped hearing Zachary chat about her favorite beverage might rest her mind.

He got out all his ingredients and set them in perfect order along the counter. "I start with dark organic cocoa. I use whole milk, raw sugar, vanilla, and then I top it with a little marshmallow cream."

Nori nodded. "Sounds good." She watched him as he puttered around the kitchen. He set out napkins and spoons on the placemats. His shoulders relaxed and that cringing expression that sometimes crossed his face had melted away. She realized he seemed different in his own home. Nori let her body relax as well. Maybe Zachary could be another friend like Blake.

When Zachary had finished his stirring and pouring, he set a steaming mug down in front of her.

She waited for him to sit down, and then she blew on the drink and took a tentative sip. Rich, dark creamy goodness rolled down her throat. Satisfying and even better than her cocoa. "It's good. And the marshmallow cream is perfect on top."

Zachary didn't try his drink but seemed to focus all his attention on Nori's reaction. "I'm glad you like it." His whole face lit up as he placed the jar of marshmallow cream in front of her. "Please, take it with you."

"Thanks." He looked pretty close to handsome when he smiled like that. Nori took another sip. The beverage was like drowning in decadence. It didn't take away the pain of the day, but it did soften the moment. Here she was, finally with a man who not only loved cocoa but who fixed her a gourmet cup. It was almost a shame to fritter away such kindness and generosity. But what could she do? Her faith in matrimony would need a great deal of nurturing. And she had no idea how many years of encouragement it would take before she could walk down that aisle.

"So, later, would you like to watch a movie?" Zachary fingered his mug, which was unexpectedly painted with monster trucks.

She could tell Zachary was trying to be nonchalant, but that flinching nervousness had come back. He seemed to be forever preparing himself for a blow like a dog that had been kicked one too many times. She looked into his eyes as he sipped his cocoa, and she saw something she hadn't noticed before. Not love, perhaps, but something serious, and something she was no longer ready to pursue. To keep from hurting him in the end, she would need to be candid. Friends, just friends. That's all she could give him.

"Zachary?"

"Yes?" His face filled with eagerness and affection.

Nori's heart ached for Zachary, since she didn't want to give him even more cause to cringe at life. But what else could she do? "I want to be honest with you." She cleared her throat. "I'm hoping we can just be. . .friends. Okay?"

twelve

Zachary lowered his gaze. When he raised his head, his expression had changed from anticipation to distress. "I understand."

A pang of guilt seized Nori. Since she, too, had known rejection over the years, it was hard not to feel his disappointment. "It's just that after today's news, dating just doesn't look as good to me as it did when I first got up this morning." She covered his hand with hers. "But then maybe you were just being a good neighbor by offering me the cocoa. Maybe I'm making too much of this." She noticed how warm and sturdy Zachary's hands were. Good hands, capable of kind deeds.

"My invitation was more than just being a good neighbor." Zachary stared at her hand.

"Thank you for your honesty." Nori knew how hard those words must have been for him to say, particularly since she hadn't returned his affection.

"When my parents got their divorce about ten years ago, I felt the same way you do now. But things changed in my mind. As time went on, the need for companionship eventually outweighed the fear of repeating my parents' mistakes." Zachary let out a breath of air like he was glad to have gotten those words out of his system.

"Yes, I can appreciate your experience, but I'm not sure when I'm going to feel like that. I've had quite a shock. And I need to work things through. It would help so much to talk to my parents. . .to understand what happened."

Zachary took a sip of his drink. "This must be very hard for you."

"It is."

He rose from his chair. "Do you want more cocoa?"

"No, but thank you. It was the best I've ever had."

He grinned at that.

Nori pushed her mug away from the edge of the table and then gave it a few more inches for good measure. Then she moved it again but wasn't sure why.

"That might get worse." Zachary looked amazed as his own comment.

"What will get worse?"

He sucked in some air and looked all around like he was frantic to change the subject. "Oh well, I was just mumbling."

Nori massaged the back of her neck. "But I want to know what you meant."

"Your compulsive disorder. It can get worse with stress, but you'll get through it. I promise." Zachary looked even more worried with his words. "I have the same problem, but we don't have to be embarrassed about it. Since we're going to be friends, I think it would be okay for us to talk about it."

Nori wasn't sure whether to be upset or inquisitive. "How did you know I have that. . .problem?"

Zachary reddened. "Well, we both leave for work about the same time each morning. I can hear you locking your door and then coming back to check it. And then talking to yourself about locking it."

Feeling suddenly vulnerable, Nori hugged herself around the middle. "Well, lots of people do that."

"Yes, but not every day. . .unless. . ." His voice died away.

"What else can you hear in my apartment?" Nori tugged on her earring, trying to appear calm.

"Not much. A little music once in a while. You like jazz,

I think. And some folk music."

"I do," Nori said. "I like that new artist in Little Rock. . . Hudson Mandel. He plays at the Silver Moon Café there." Nori thought changing the topic might be easier on her already tense emotions. "I heard him about a year ago when I was in Little Rock. Have you heard him?"

Zachary shook his head. "No. Haven't had the pleasure."

After a moment of silence and a few seconds to rethink her change of subject, Nori thought maybe discussing their disorder might be a relief instead of a strain. They were, as he just affirmed, friends who should be able to talk without censor. "So, you've got obsessive-compulsive disorder, too?"

Zachary nodded.

"Do you know how you got it? The OCD?" It was hard for Nori not to be curious. She'd never known anyone else with the disorder.

Zachary took in a lungful of air. "I can't remember one defining moment when I suddenly had OCD. The problem came on gradually. My guess is that it came on from a buildup of a lot of little things." He tensed his fingers around his mug until his knuckles were white.

"I see." In spite of her own problems, Nori found herself concerned about his life. Instead of asking him more specific questions, she decided just to wait and listen.

Zachary cleared his throat. "I think people get the idea that if they're careful enough about everything no one can hurt them. But that's ridiculous." He looked at her. "The only way not to be hurt in this life is to be dead."

Nori chuckled and then felt her face get hot. "Oh, I'm sorry I laughed. That wasn't funny. It just surprised me to hear you put it that way." She hoped her new stance on dating hadn't worsened his problem.

"But I've kept my problem under control well enough that

I've never needed medicine or therapy. What about you?"

"What do you mean?" Nori asked.

"Your compulsive behavior? Do you know when it started?"

"Oh, well, I've never known for sure. The first time I noticed the problem was in grade school. I'd forgotten to take my homework to school, and I freaked out about it. I wanted to impress the teachers, and getting a zero on my homework was more than my little heart could take. Anyway, after that, I started checking my backpack. Then I'd wonder later if I'd *really* looked, so then I'd say out loud, 'I have my homework in the bag.' That sort of thing. You probably know what I mean." The memory made Nori flinch as she recalled the misery of always checking things.

Zachary nodded. "Yeah, I know exactly what you mean."

"And then this pattern of behavior started seeping into other areas of my life. But it's kind of like yours. I can dismiss it often enough that it hasn't been a great hindrance. Just a little pesky at times." She attempted a weak smile.

Zachary made no gestures of disgust or surprise. He just seemed to be listening. That part felt really good to Nori.

"I guess I should be going." She rose.

"Okay."

Nori waited for Zachary to protest, but he didn't. She appreciated the fact that he'd kept his promise not to pressure her into staying longer than she wanted to. *Good man.*

As she made her way out of the kitchen and through the living room, she happened to see herself in a mirror. She stopped cold. Raccoon smudges of mascara circled her eyes, and spikes of hair shot up around her face like palm fronds in a hurricane. And her dress was still soiled with cherry juice. "I look terrible. Why didn't you say something?"

Zachary looked puzzled at her comment. "Because you don't look terrible. In fact, you look wonderful."

Well, he's either blind or lying. Or maybe he was just being kind. "Thanks for the cocoa."

As Zachary walked Nori to the front door, she felt her heart beat out of rhythm. It pounded hard and then skipped some beats. She placed her hand over her chest.

"Are you okay?" Zachary asked.

"My heart. I feel funny."

"Here, rest over here." Zachary led her to the couch, and she sat down. "Do you need for me to call 911?"

Nori shook her head. "No, I just need to rest for a minute." She stretched out on the couch, hoping the odd sensations would pass. "I'm sorry to be so much trouble."

Zachary knelt beside her. "It's no trouble at all." Without faltering, he took hold of her hand and squeezed.

A tingle, unexpected and warm, trickled through her. In spite of herself, she squeezed back. Then she noticed it—Zachary no longer looked downward but gazed straight into her eyes. And those eyes. . .they were the same color of the chocolate-covered coffee beans he loved so much.

He released her hand and sat on the chair next to her. "Maybe it was the stress of the day. Some sleep would do you good."

Nori studied Zachary's face. He seemed more confident than usual. She liked it. It felt safe somehow. "Yes, sleep. I need to go home. I should be home." Even as she said those words, she could feel herself getting uncontrollably drowsy. Her mind continued to float until her eyelids became heavy. Soon she was overcome with sleepy thoughts and pleasant things, so she followed them. Maybe she'd let herself doze off for just a moment. . . .

❧

Zachary watched Nori as she drifted off, thinking how lovely and peaceful she looked. But he wondered what he should do. Let her sleep until morning? Wake her up in an hour so she could go home? He had no idea.

He thought of Nori's comment about being no more than friends. The idea pierced him through, and yet she had indeed sustained quite a blow with her parents' sudden plans for divorce. But would she ever change her mind? Perhaps Nori would never love him. In spite of the opposing arguments, he would be a dependable friend to her. No matter what.

He picked up *Fields of Amber Light,* which he'd been reading in short intervals, and started where he'd left off:

The wait became a desolate winter. I loved her, and I could no longer live without her gaze, her hand brushing my cheek, or the pledge my heart ached to give her. How would I endure these cold days of March, these days of never-ending sorrow?

After a few more minutes of reading, Zachary closed the book again. The words seemed too close. Too real. The only way he could handle the story was to read it in small increments, though he couldn't help but hope the author had written a happy ending.

Zachary gazed over at Nori. Her breathing intensified to a light snore. He grinned. She was so close to him just now, and yet soon she'd rise and leave. *And she might never come back.* He admonished himself, thinking how unwise it might have been to tell her about his OCD. Would the admission make him look more human or wimpy? Probably the latter. He didn't know women well enough to know what pleased or repelled them. And yet, if they were friends, true friends, couldn't they discuss anything?

Nori stretched her head back. "Please, no," she said in her sleep. "Why?"

She's having a nightmare. Zachary touched the sleeve of her dress.

"Nori?"

"What?" She roused, looking around. "Where am I?" Her brows furrowed.

"You're in my apartment." Zachary wanted to take her into his arms and comfort her, but knowing how unwelcome that would be, he just waited by her side.

Nori glanced at him. "I guess I was pretty tired. Sorry."

"There's no reason to apologize."

"Was I talking in my sleep?" She sat up.

"Yes."

Nori rubbed her neck and smiled. "Did I reveal any dark secrets?"

"You were having a nightmare." Zachary leaned toward her.

"I guess I was—about my parents." Nori looked at him. "Thank you for being so kind to me, Zachary Martin." She took his hand and gave it a squeeze.

If there were such a thing as a body blush, Zachary thought he just might have had one. He never knew when Nori was suddenly going to render him speechless.

She released his hand and looked at his book. "I do love that title. *Fields of Amber Light.* How is it?"

"Good."

"Would you read a few lines out loud? It's like candy for the mind. . .with no calories."

Zachary chuckled. He let the novel open in a random spot and began to read again:

"The cold air warmed the instant I saw her face. She had chosen to surprise me, and surprise me she did. My whole being rose like the eastern sun, and I kissed her smiling face.

"You brought spring with you. Shall we celebrate?" she asked.
"I know of a field that just might remember us." I said.
"But this time, we should dance to a wedding song."

Zachary stopped before his voice betrayed his emotions.

"Thank you." Nori seemed to study his face as she rose from the couch. "My heart feels fine now. And I guess I'd better not trample on your hospitality any longer."

If only you knew. I wish you could stay forever. But Nori didn't know that. She only thought he'd wanted a date. "It's been a pleasure. Well, not the part about your unhappy news or the flutters in your heart. But just you. . .being here."

Nori smiled and walked to the door.

Zachary followed her, feeling his own "desolate winter" coming on. The chance of her ever coming back for cocoa was as likely as seeing Halley's Comet. *Why does love have to be so complicated?*

The time they'd spent together at the bookshop seemed surreal and wonderful. He hadn't even known he was capable of being so happy. For a moment, he'd lived something truly amazing. But it had only lasted for a moment.

"Thanks. . .for everything," Nori said. "Good-bye."

Why did she always have to say good-bye like they'd never see each other again? "Good night, Nori. Come over anytime you're in need of a friend or some cocoa."

She touched his face. "You are so dear."

Zachary watched her until she'd gone into her apartment for the night. He placed his hand on his cheek. On the very spot she'd just touched. His skin heated up—considerably—and he wondered about the chemical reactions. Surely if he could explicate these sensations, he would be more immune to them. He chuckled, wondering if love was no more than a combination of compounds colliding. And yet, there were so many irregularities, too—things science would never be able to fully explain.

He pulled out the *Courtship for Idiots* book from behind the curtain and set it out on the entry table to remind him to glance through it one more time. He wouldn't allow the advice to rule his life, but he thought it still might be good for a tip or two. Just as he was making his way to the bedroom, he heard a loud rap at the door. *Nori?* He headed back to the door and opened it.

Nori stood in front of him again, smiling. "I forgot my marshmallow cream."

"That's right." Zachary retrieved the jar and handed it to her, wishing he could think of something to prolong her stay.

"Thanks." She held up the jar. "I promise I'll use it." Nori pointed to the book on his entry table. "Oh, I see you've got the book *Courtship for Idiots.*"

Zachary's face blazed with the heat of a hundred red-hot suns. *So much for controlling chemical reactions.*

thirteen

Nori realized she should have kept her observation about the book to herself. *I'd better put him out of his misery.* "I saw that courtship book at the store, too." She offered her sincerest smile. "I ended up buying *Finding Your Dreamboat* instead. Totally worthless, though. I intend to use it for kindling." She chuckled, thinking how liberating it felt to no longer hide things from the opposite sex. No more reason for airs if one wasn't actively pursuing a husband. All could be given openly without worry of repercussions or rejection.

"Really?" Zachary asked. "I guess some parts of life are confusing. I figured a little help wouldn't hurt."

"Well, when you come across the right woman, Zachary, self-help books will be useless. I hear love erases all need for formulas. At least that's what my mother *used* to say." She sighed and said good night.

As she left Zachary, she saw such intensity in his eyes. Had she upset him in some way? Had he loved once and lost? She breathed a prayer for her friend and walked to the front door, clutching her keys and his jar of marshmallow cream.

When Nori had readied herself for bed and slipped under the covers, she realized she felt a little more at peace. Zachary really had been a friend to her in a time of need. Her parents' divorce still seemed shocking and unbelievable, and yet she was calm enough to consider the news in a more reasonable way.

As Nori drifted off, she wondered if she'd dream about

Zachary again. When she was resting on his couch, one of her dreams had been about him—it was the one dream she hadn't mentioned to him.

Much later, while enjoying her deep slumbers, Nori heard a noise. She jolted up in bed. What was that? *The telephone.* She shook off her sleep and glanced at the clock. 1:10 a.m. After another ring, she picked up the phone. "Hello?"

"Noreen?"

"Mother? Is that you? Are you okay? Where are—"

"I'm downstairs."

"What?"

"I couldn't remember if your apartment number was 203 or 205." Her mother sounded exhausted.

"It's 203. I can't believe you're here. I'm glad." Nori reminded herself to breathe.

"My flight was exhausting, but after I got home I wasn't able to sleep. Thought I'd drive over to see you."

All the way from Forrest City in the middle of the night? "Come on up. I'll see you in a minute." She threw on her fluffiest robe and scurried around the apartment, trying to make things tidy.

They hadn't seen each other in a long while, so Nori wanted their reunion to be lovely in every way. And yet that was impossible now, since she wasn't sure how she could avoid a confrontation about the upcoming divorce.

Nori tightened her robe. She loved her mother and she'd always dreamed of a close relationship, but for some reason it had always eluded them. In high school, they'd connected when she'd won an award in home economics. Her mother had seemed so proud of her when a local reporter came to the house to interview her. Nori had experienced a brief and wonderful attachment to her mom that week. In fact, it had been the best week of her life. But no matter how hard they had both tried since then, something always seemed to come between them.

The doorbell rang, jolting Nori from her daydream. She ran to the door, and with her hands trembling, she opened it.

Her mother stood in the hallway, still tall and stout, but looking weary-eyed and older. "Hello," she said.

"Hi." Nori stepped into the hallway and gathered her mother into a hug. She smelled of baby powder, a scent Nori had almost forgotten.

Her mother pulled away first, and then she patted her daughter on the back. "Well, it's been a long time."

"Yes. Too long." Nori picked up her mother's suitcase and led her into the apartment.

"My, my, my." She looked around, shaking her head. "I'd forgotten how nice your apartment was. *And* how expensive it must be."

Nori hated for her mother to think that she was wasting money, especially since she lived well within her means. But to keep from sounding defensive, she said, "The shop is doing very well."

"Oh really." Her mother raised an eyebrow. "That *is* good. I'm sure your *grandmother* would have been pleased." She picked at the material on her pantsuit.

"Yes." Nori stuffed her hands into the pockets of her robe, already wondering what she could say next.

"Funny, after all this time, and considering what you do, I've never known what your favorite candy is." Her mother seemed to wait for an answer.

"Well, actually there is one candy that I love above all others. It's—"

"Oh boy, do I need to take a load off." Her mother eased

onto the sofa, leaned against the back of the couch, and closed her eyes.

Nori sat down next to her. *Poor Mom.* "You know, maybe tomorrow afternoon we could go to one of the spas. I think you'd really enjoy it. Everything they do is so rejuvenating. And it'll be my treat."

Surely she wasn't asleep already. Couldn't tell. But her mother had so many times tuned her out simply by shutting her eyes. "By the way, I can sleep out here, and you may have my bed."

"Thank you, dear."

Nori sighed. So she wasn't asleep. "Are you hungry? Or maybe you'd like something to drink. Chamomile might help you to rest."

Her mother raised her head, looking bleary-eyed. "Maybe some good strong coffee. I've still got jet lag."

Strong coffee? Nori couldn't imagine how loads of caffeine just before bed would help with jet lag, but she headed to the kitchen anyway.

Nori counted out the scoops of coffee, but then when she was finished, she wasn't sure how many she'd put in the paper cone. She poured the granules back in the package and started over. After several more attempts, she poured the water over the granules and turned on the machine. *Finally.* She marveled how she could even run a candy shop with such an annoying and time-consuming disorder. But for some reason the only time her compulsiveness became truly unmanageable was when she was with her mother. Nori breathed a quick prayer for strength. When the coffee machine beeped, her mother came through the door and sat down at the kitchen table.

For a moment Nori felt helpless, wondering what to do with the elephant in the room that they were both trying so hard to ignore—the upcoming divorce. What could she say that wouldn't start an argument?

"I know what your quiet is all about," her mother said. "I just want you to know, we both agreed to the divorce." She crossed her arms. "Nobody's hurting."

But what about me? I'm hurting. Nori kept her face toward the cabinets. She pressed her finger against her lips to help keep her emotions in check. "But why, Mom? Why now, after decades of marriage?"

"I'm really sorry." Her mother stared into space.

"But I thought you and Dad were happy." How could she have misunderstood all those years? "Were you only pretending all that time?" Nori gripped the edge of the counter until her fingers throbbed.

"Your father and I didn't want you growing up in a broken home." She raised her hands. "Now, I'm not blaming you. I'm just saying you're grown now. You've got a good career. And, well, we need to move on."

Her mother had said the words as if she were talking about hiring a new lawn service. Her casual and detached manner angered Nori. Trying to control her emotions, she busied herself by setting out cream and sugar and pouring them each a cup of coffee. There were a thousand things to say, and yet she wasn't sure what to ask first.

They sat for a while, sipping from their cups and chatting about the brand and flavor of the coffee. While they talked about everything and nothing, Nori took note of other changes in her mother. Her green eyes had lost some of their gleam, and her blond tresses showed hints of gray. But most noticeable was the change in her mother's temperament, which was now more tentative and melancholy.

When all the light chitchat had played itself out, they fell into silence.

In spite of the distress she felt for her mother, Nori could stand the wait no longer. "I'm sure you know. . .I have questions. I really—"

"I'm sure you do, dear." Pain shadowed her mother's face. "But I'm awfully tired right now. If you don't mind, I'm going to bed." She jerked up from the table, making the chair fall backward against the tile.

When Nori came to her mother's aid, she saw the sadness in her eyes and the tremor in her fingers. "Are you sure you're—"

"We'll feel better in the morning. Won't we?" Her mother's voice sounded hoarse with emotion.

Nori decided to let the anxious moment unwind. "You're right."

Her mother rinsed the cups and set them in the sink.

She hoped her mother was right—that after a good night's sleep, things would look better in the morning. Or at least clearer.

And yet, her mother's expression left her with a sense of dread. Was something else wrong? Perhaps something her mother was still hiding from her?

❧

Nori woke with a start. Then she remembered she'd slept on the couch. The night had been riddled with night sweats and dreadful dreams. And the couch had been lumpy and the blankets itchy. Not a good combo.

She glanced over at the wall clock. 7:12 a.m. She rose from the couch feeling stiff and miserable. She rubbed her stomach, which still felt sour from the late night coffee.

Before showering, Nori padded into the bedroom to check on her mom. She stared at the empty bed and the rumpled sheets. "Mother?" Nori looked in the master bath. Empty as well. The sense of dread she'd felt the night before washed over her. She ran through the whole apartment, flicking on all the lights as she went, but the reality had already hit. Her mother was gone.

fourteen

Nori checked the front door. Her mother had closed it, but she'd left it unlocked. *Glad my apartment building is a safe place.*

She opened the door and looked down the hallway. No one was there. All quiet. Maybe her mother had just run to the store for a few toiletries and hadn't wanted to disturb her sleep. But even as she thought it, she knew something else was at play.

She went into the kitchen, and while pouring herself some orange juice, she noticed a note next to the vase of flowers. She picked up the note and read it:

> *Noreen,*
> *I'm going on a cruise, so I had to get up early. Sorry I left before saying good-bye, but I thought things might be easier this way.*
>
> *Love, Mom*

The note fell from Nori's hand. She hadn't seen her mother in ages, and now she'd vanished again. When would they ever get to talk? Not just dance around their real feelings with coffee chatter. Nori had hoped they could get to know each other better over the next few days. Find some common ground. Maybe talk about the Lord or friends or anything. Then maybe once they'd formed a closer bond, perhaps her mother would feel comfortable enough to explain the whys of the sudden break-up of her marriage.

Nori eased to the floor and let her head fall back against the cabinets. All this time, she'd naively thought her parents were busy enjoying the beginnings of their golden years: traveling, gardening, and learning to cook together. What a crock that was. She picked up her mother's note again and stared at it, trying to discover any nuances or hidden meanings.

Then Nori groaned, remembering her own questions as well as an accusation or two. Instead of waiting patiently for her mother to talk about the divorce as she'd hoped to do, she'd started the inquisition too soon. But what had she expected her to say with such shocking news—"I'm happy for you?"

The tears came. She clutched her nightgown like a lifeline, hoping for some reprieve. None came. She shook her head at romance and marriage and love. What kind of dreamworld had she been living in?

Oh, God, please, I need Your help. And my parents do, too. Please guide them in all things, even if they don't want Your help.

She reached into the pantry, snatched a wad of napkins off a shelf, and blew her nose. After a shower and some whole grain toast, she dragged herself out the front door. She couldn't imagine greeting customers in her foul state of mind, but it had to be done.

Zachary emerged from his apartment.

Oh no. She wasn't even in the mood for friends. "Hi."

"Hi there." Zachary cleared his throat. "I wanted to let you know I'm going to be gone for a little while."

Nori turned to him. "Gone?" Why was everybody leaving?

He caught up with her. "Well, I won this. . .this award, and so I need to go to a banquet."

"An award? What kind?"

"Geophysicist of the year." He blushed.

"You mean statewide?" Nori tried to act interested. She might be feeling as low as dirt, but she wasn't going to hurt Zachary's feelings.

"No." He looked away. "It's a. . .national award."

Nori's mouth fell open. "That's incredible. Congratulations."

Zachary smiled. "That means a lot to me. I mean, you saying that. Thanks."

She had to admit, his humility seemed real as well as endearing. Most people she knew would take kudos like that and make the most of it—like mentioning it coolly every few seconds. "So where do you fly off to?"

"Denver. I'll be gone about two weeks."

"Oh?" *Two weeks?* Nori felt disappointed. She hadn't expected that much sentiment. Her eyes misted over, but she squelched her emotions before they could be detected.

"I haven't had a vacation in five years, so I thought it'd be nice to do some hiking while I was in Colorado."

"Do you hike a lot?"

"I've been hiking every weekend for a while now." He grinned. "I'd like to expand my horizons."

"That sounds good." Nori locked her door. "Why didn't you mention the award yesterday evening?"

Zachary fiddled with his picture ID, which dangled from his belt loop. "Well, with the news you got yesterday, it didn't seem like the right time to mention it."

How selfless was that? Nori tried not to stare at this man named Zachary. She was lucky to have him for a friend. "Thank you."

"You're welcome. Do you feel better today?"

Nori wanted to pour her heart out to him, but she knew it would take all day. Maybe all year. And she didn't want Lizza to think she'd abandoned her at the shop. "Not totally. My mother showed up last night, but we didn't get a chance to talk very much. At least not about anything important. And then she left early this morning for a cruise."

"I'm sorry." Zachary moved toward her. "I can cancel my

trip if you need me. You know, as a friend."

"Cancel? Oh no. Your award. I would never ask you to do that."

Zachary smiled. "Well, that's what friends do."

Yes, it *was* what friends did, or so she'd heard. Nori had never known anyone within the male persuasion, or anyone for that matter, who possessed such a noble heart. "I'll be okay. But I *really* appreciate the offer." She reached out and touched his arm.

Zachary nodded, looking embarrassed but pleased.

They rode the elevator together and then, after a heartfelt good-bye, went their separate ways.

Nori drove to work, gathered up her courage, and hauled herself into Sweet Nothings. Lizza was ready for business and looked chipper, as always. Nori shook her head, feeling disappointed and hurt over all the recent events. One minute she had her act together, and then the next it was like somebody had tossed the pieces of her life in a bag, shaken them up, and then dumped them on the ground. What a mess.

"S'up? You look like you need a handful of jelly beans. Doctor's orders." Lizza winked.

"No thanks. I'm not hungry, but I do have a story to tell you. A lot has happened. Too much, in fact." Where in the world would she begin? With Blake or Zachary or her parents' divorce? She took in a deep breath and began her tale.

While they worked, dipping strawberries in molten chocolate, Nori continued with her dismal highlights. "Anyway, Zachary and I are just going to be good friends. And I think that's a good thing."

Nori didn't dare ask for her friend's opinion, especially since the date with Blake had gone so strangely. But she could tell Lizza was busting with queries. And advice. Nori cleared her throat. "And my parents are getting a divorce."

Lizza froze, her strawberry still poised in midair. "Excuse me? Your parents are getting a *what?*"

"A divorce." The words still seemed impossible to Nori.

"Oh no. But this cannot be." Lizza set her berry on the wax paper and placed her hands on her hips. "But I thought they had—"

"I know, we both thought they had a good marriage, but apparently they didn't."

"It's so hard to believe." Lizza gave Nori's back a gentle rub. "I'm so sorry. Oh, but the word 'sorry' gets used for every little thing, doesn't it? I wish I had a better word." Lizza placed her palm over her heart. "I feel a better word right here."

"Thanks. Really." Nori took in a deep breath as she went back to dipping the strawberries into the chocolate.

❧

After a day at work that felt more like a month, Nori trudged back home. She slid onto the couch and let her mind hash through all that she'd kept at bay. Questions, one after another, poured out until she felt like she was drowning in them.

Just as Nori began sharing her troubles with God, she heard a soft tapping at the front door. *Mom?*

Nori found Zachary standing at her door. "When is your flight?"

"Early tomorrow morning."

"Do you want to come in?" Nori hoped he'd say yes, even though moping for a while sounded pretty comforting, too.

Zachary shook his head. "That's okay. I just wanted to give you this." He offered her a book.

Nori accepted the gift—a rich brown journal trimmed in gold.

"It's a journal," he said. "You know, for writing things down. Important things and. . .well. . .not so important things. I use one all the time, and it helps me. I can better see where I've been and where I want to go. When I like life and when I hate it." He grinned. "That sort of thing."

Nori noticed Zachary's relaxed demeanor as he talked about journaling. She was fond of him like that—when he stopped trying so hard and was just being himself. Her fingers traced the gold trim. "It's beautiful. And the most thoughtful thing anyone has ever given me."

Zachary nodded, looking pleased.

Nori no longer kept her expression in check but let a smile warm her face. With the pressure off to constantly be on a manhunt, she could allow herself to unwind a little. Then she could spend all her excess time worrying about her parents.

"Well, bye," Zachary suddenly said.

"Good-bye." Nori didn't want to, but she let him go. "Have a safe trip." She closed the door and sat back down on the couch, taking in the beauty of the leather-bound journal. She lifted the heavy cover and noticed a sticky note on the first page. The note contained a quote by Ralph Waldo Emerson—*"A friend may well be reckoned the masterpiece of nature."* Nice saying. *Really* nice.

Nori flipped through the rest of the journal. Each page appeared to have a note with either a quote or a scripture. Zachary had taken the time to write out words of encouragement. Nori shook her head, smiling. *Amazing.* She already knew what her first entry would be: *"I don't deserve a friend like Zachary Martin."*

The doorbell rang, and she found herself hoping it was Zachary. When she opened the door, Blake stood in the hallway sporting a toothy grin, a denim shirt, and a few flips of freshly highlighted hair. "Howdy-do."

"Hi," Nori said, trying not to show her disappointment. "What are you doing here?"

Blake leaned on the door frame. "Wow, you look thinner or something."

"Thanks." Why, why, why, she wondered, was Blake always leaning on everything? And why did it bother her so much?

"Well, hey, I hadn't seen you in a while, and I was in the neighborhood. So I thought maybe you'd like to share a meal with me since you're going to be my sister."

Nori took in some much-needed oxygen. "I'd love to, but I need to stay home tonight."

"That's okay. Maybe I could go buy us some groceries and we could fix it right here. But I have to warn you, I'm one lousy cook." Blake lowered his head in mock shame.

"So am I."

"No way."

"Yeah, I'm afraid I'm a typical single, too. I'm a terrible cook, and all I have in my fridge right now is orange juice, a carton of expired milk, and some veggies that are one stage away from penicillin." She shot him her chirpiest smile, trying to imagine what in the world Blake would say to that.

"But I'm allergic to penicillin."

Nori chuckled, but then she realized he wasn't joking.

Blake just stared at her. "Uh, I thought all you gals stocked food supplies and were good at cooking and stuff. Weren't you all kind of born that way?" He waggled his eyebrows.

"Not really. Are all you guys born with the know-how to replace a car muffler?"

"Well, *I* sure can't. That's why I have a good mechanic." He donned a sheepish grin. "Oh, I get it. I think you're just trying to say no. That's okay. Maybe another time."

Blake had such a dejected look that she felt sorry for him. "You're welcome to come in for a bit. I could make cocoa."

"Naw. I've never liked hot chocolate. Makes me think of what ladies drink when they're old and lonely." His expression warped into panic. "Oww, boy. Guess that came off bad. Sorry. I hope I didn't hurt your feelings."

"No. You're fine." Nori grinned.

"I'd better get going." He stuffed his hands in his pockets.

"Thanks for dropping by."

"Same to you." Blake gave her a big-eyed grin and then meandered down the hallway toward the elevator.

What was that all about? Nori closed the door. Was Blake's spiel just a weaseling way to get her to fix supper for him? Had that been the real reason he'd asked her to be his sister? Maybe not. Maybe she was just seeing the worst possible scenario since she was tired enough to sleep under the sink.

Nori decided to go to bed before somebody else showed up for a seven-course meal or a back rub or maybe some free financial planning.

fifteen

Over the next two weeks, Nori threw herself into her work at Sweet Nothings, worked out at the gym with rabid determination, and found herself losing some of her fascination with food. She guessed it was one of the benefits of despair.

Her father hadn't returned her calls to talk about the divorce, so she assumed he was lying low in fear that their conversation would turn into a moral debate. She was in no mood for a quarrel, so she let the confrontation go. For now.

Nori milled around the shop doing all the usual things, but her thoughts were elsewhere. Zachary had been gone for two whole weeks and a day, and Nori realized that was part of the problem. She missed her friend.

Feeling preoccupied and lonesome, Nori thought some fresh air and window-shopping might do her some good. So, during her lunch break, she ambled out of Sweet Nothings and then strolled along the sidewalk on Central Avenue, gazing at the shops and pretending to be one of the tourists. She never tired of the town's old-world quaintness and its eclectic mixture of architecture.

A crystal chandelier in an antique shop caught Nori's attention. She thought the fixture would look stunning in a big dining room. But that couldn't happen without buying a home of her own since her apartment dining room wasn't very big or formal. And the landlord probably wouldn't appreciate her changing all the light fixtures. The yearning to settle her life in a more permanent situation tugged at her heart. She had to admit that in spite of what her parents were going through, she still longed for a home and family.

Nori continued walking past hotels, art studios, restaurants, and bathhouses and then made her way back to Arlington Lawn at The Promenade. She stood in her beloved spot, looking over the hot springs, hoping the waters and the sun's warmth could revive her. It always astonished her that she lived and worked next to a national park.

She leaned over the railing and watched the rising steam curl into ribbons while the rest of the thermal waters tumbled over the boulders. Nature's music. The sights and sounds were simple blessings but ones she was deeply grateful for. And especially now in early spring. . .when everything seemed to affirm and declare that God was still in the business of caring for all He'd created.

Nori took in the view of the historic district, the verdant hills cradling the town, the stately magnolia trees, and the many families below dipping their feet in the thermal waters. The village had always made her think of something magical, especially now with all the blooming flowers. *I could never live anywhere else. Spoiled for life, I guess.*

Her mind drifted to other fine things. Zachary. She wondered when he'd fly in. And against her better judgment, she began to compare Blake and Zachary. Both were so very different. God had never made the same man twice—that was certain.

She thought of the first time she truly "saw" Zachary—when he'd ditched his glasses and his wrinkled clothes. *Oh dear.* She felt a familiar twinge of guilt. *I didn't notice Zachary until he'd made himself "pretty."* She lowered her head, thinking how shallow and predictably human she was. And yet, somehow he cared for her. Deeply. Perhaps even unwisely.

Someone caught her attention out of the corner of her eye. The man who'd filled her head and heart was walking straight toward her.

Zachary.

sixteen

Zachary took in the wonder of Nori. She looked all gorgeous in a pair of black jeans and a gauzy blouse. How wonderful she looked—had always looked. And she was standing in his favorite spot, smiling at him. Did life get any better? He moved toward her. "Hello."

Nori made up the distance between them, hugging him. "I'm glad to see you."

Okay, that was better than he'd hoped. So much better. Zachary returned Nori's embrace. She felt soft and warm against him, and as he imagined, she smelled of all things sweet. Then, suddenly, the moment was over and they released each other.

"How did you know I'd be here?"

"I stopped by the shop. Lizza told me."

Nori clasped her hands together. "So, tell me about this award."

"Well, it's etched in green glass. It's nice. I'll show it to you sometime."

"Was there a big crowd? Did you have an acceptance speech?" Nori's voice sounded a little breathless.

"There were about six hundred people at the banquet, and I said I was pleased to receive the award. That was about it." Zachary chuckled. "I was a little nervous."

"I would have been, too."

"Really?"

Nori nodded. "And did you go hiking while you were in Colorado?"

"Yeah. It was great." He rested his arms against the railing and looked out over the town. "There's a quiet about it that gets to you. Makes me more attentive to the things I usually ignore. And then the sounds and sights and smells suddenly seem. . .well. . .miraculous."

Nori stared at him with a new expression—one he hadn't seen on her before. Somewhere between astonishment and delight. He liked it. A lot.

"Hmm. Sounds like an excellent pastime. And it burns calories." She smiled. "I've always needed a good hobby, but I just haven't. . ." Her voice trailed off before starting again. "So is that where you got your tan?"

"Mostly from the skiing. It's a—"

"You went skiing, too?" Nori looked surprised.

"Yeah. I love the hiking, but I have to admit the skiing is a little. . .unpredictable."

Nori chuckled. "Yes, it certainly is."

"But it was good for me. . .to try something out of my comfort zone. By the way, there are a bunch of good hiking trails around here. Maybe you'd like to go with me sometime." *Wow, that was pretty bold.* Usually after a statement like that he'd plummet headlong into an abyss of mortification. Instead, he decided to smile.

"Okay. That sounds nice."

"Good." He hated to spoil a perfect moment by asking about the divorce, but he wondered how Nori was doing. "So, how have you been?"

"I'm still pretty confused and hurt about my parents' divorce. But I'm dealing with it. . .one day at a time." She looked at him. "Thank you for asking."

A family with cameras and lots of enthusiasm marched up the stairs toward them. The children were chattering about the thermal waters while their parents took snapshots. One of the children, a little girl with auburn ringlets, reached up and took hold of Nori's hand.

"Hi," Nori said to the girl.

The girl glanced up at Nori with a look of terror and then scampered back to find her mother.

"Guess she needs to pay more attention whose hand she's holding," Nori whispered to Zachary.

"Kids. They're a little random and messy," he said in a low voice. "But I'd like to have a few anyway."

Nori chuckled as she seemed to study him. "Well, I'd better get back to work. I'd hate to make Lizza think I've deserted her. Why don't you drop by the shop later for something sweet? It'll be on the house."

"I'll try not to choke this time."

"That's good. I prefer my customers go away happy. . .and still breathing."

They chuckled and then walked down the steps toward the street.

Zachary wondered what it would feel like to reach out and take her hand like the girl had. He imagined the experience would be intensely satisfying, though he didn't discount the perilous side of such an exploit. All the things that could go awry. . . And yet Zachary wished he could toss caution to the wind and simply reach out to her.

❧

The second his watch read 5:00 p.m., Zachary rose from his desk and sprinted out to his car. In five minutes, give or take a few seconds, he'd be in the presence of Nori. The thrill of seeing her again, especially now that she didn't loathe him, outweighed anything he'd ever done—watching *Star Trek* marathons or meeting his favorite science fiction authors or even going hiking in his favorite places. Nori surpassed all things wonderful.

In a burst of confidence, Zachary sped over to Sweet Nothings, strode to the shop, and threw open the door.

Nori said good-bye to several customers, and then she locked eyes with him.

Nice.

Almost on cue, Lizza disappeared into the back room.

Nori strolled over to Zachary. "Well, do you see something you would like?" she asked with a sweep of her hand.

Zachary tugged on his collar and blinked. If she only knew. "Well, how about some maple sugar cakes? Those are always good."

"What an interesting selection." Nori tapped her finger against her cheek.

"Does it mean anything?"

"Yes, I think so. Women rarely buy it. Maple sugar candies are usually purchased by men who like the outdoors. Men who are comfortable with themselves. The discerning man."

Zachary straightened his shoulders. He was feeling better by the minute. "Really? You can tell all that from maple sugar? I guess I just thought I liked the flavor."

"Candy is a very individual thing." Nori raised her chin. "People take their sweets very seriously."

Zachary had no idea there was so much study behind the selection of candy.

Nori took out a few small boxes of maple sugar cakes, placed them in a decorative Sweet Nothings box, and held it out to Zachary. "There you are. Candy collected from the finest maple trees in Vermont. Enjoy."

"Thank you."

Their hands touched in midair. Zachary felt a warm rush. In case his face looked ridiculously red, he glanced away at a row of candy bins. "I see you have plenty of chocolate-covered coffee beans on hand."

"Well, we do try to remember what our customers like." Nori smiled. "You know, it's that personal touch that's so important."

Yes, without a doubt, Zachary liked the personal touch. "I'm sure they've come to appreciate it."

"Who appreciates what?" Lizza said, bustling back into the room with a huge bag of taffy. "Spit it out. I must know everything."

"We were just talking about getting to know our customers and what they like."

"And what they don't even know they like. . .yet." Lizza winked. "Hi, Zachary."

"Hello there."

"Listen, I've got something I need to ask you both," Lizza said. "My sister's wedding is tomorrow evening. And she said they had a few cancellations for dinner and she hated to waste the food." Lizza turned to Nori. "Anyway, she wondered if you would like to attend. It'll be a lovely wedding with an elegant dinner. Oh, and she said you could bring a date. So that means you could invite Zachary."

Right at that moment, Zachary would like to have given Lizza a thousand dollars. He looked at Nori to gauge her response. She looked a bit green, if women could be that color.

"Well, that's a thought." Nori hesitated. "But a very good thought."

He noticed Nori giving Lizza one of the female gestures that only women could decode, so he couldn't tell if that was a good sign or bad sign. But he knew he wouldn't push it. This had to be her decision.

Nori approached Zachary with a girlish grin, which made his heart feel like it was hammering itself into pieces. "Would you like to go to the wedding with me. . .as my dear friend?" she asked.

Zachary nodded with eagerness while trying not to come off too dorky. He hoped her "friends only" position would evolve into something more through the evening, and the word *dear* did sound promising.

"Okay." Nori turned to Lizza. "We'd love to accept your sister's invitation."

"It's 7:00 tomorrow evening at Forrest Heights Chapel. And then afterward, there'll be a reception and dinner. Well, I'm glad that's settled. I'll see you guys there."

"Say, shouldn't you be getting ready for the rehearsal?" Nori asked.

"No problem. It's at seven-thirty. Plenty of time." Lizza went toward the back room again, whistling a merry tune.

"I hope that didn't pressure you into something you didn't want to do," Zachary said to Nori in a low voice.

She shook her head. "Not at all. It just surprised me. I've never even met Lizza's sister. I'm sure she invited me because Lizza works with me, but still, it was very nice of her."

Zachary took a peek at his box of maple candies, thinking of the hands that put them there. Then he gazed over at her. "I've only been to two weddings. And they were a long time ago."

"Really?"

"How many have you been to?"

"Quite a few," Nori said. "I think you'll enjoy yourself."

"I know I will." Zachary tried to keep the amorous tones from his voice. "What are we supposed to wear?"

"You can wear a nice suit. But I think I'll go to the mall tomorrow morning and find a new dress."

Zachary saw the light in her eyes. He was glad for the wedding invitation, not only for himself but for Nori. He thought it might give her a rest from worrying about her parents' divorce. And it wouldn't hurt for her to see a couple deeply in love—a sight that might inspire her to think beyond friendship.

A group of noisy and hungry-looking customers suddenly barreled into the shop like a herd of buffalo.

"I'd better let you take care of your customers. I know where Forrest Heights Chapel is. I'll be by your apartment at 6:30. Is that good?" Zachary asked.

"*Very* good."

Zachary left the shop in such good spirits that he ate every one of the maple sugar cakes. Then the rest of the day whirled by.

He found a suit that seemed to be a good style and fit even though the price was astonishing. It didn't matter, though. He could afford the extra cost, and he would do anything to sweep Nori off her feet.

Did men really do that? He was a little concerned about expectations on a date. He hadn't had a date in so long he wasn't sure what to do. Was he supposed to buy Nori a corsage, or were those outdated? He had no idea.

Maybe it was best they were going as friends for now. It did indeed take some of the pressure off. In the end he decided not to buy her a corsage since it might make her look like a member of the wedding party.

When Zachary had spent more hours grooming himself than he had in his whole life, he looked at the clock. 6:29. The time had come.

He locked his apartment and walked down the hall to Nori's door. He forced his hand to stop shaking as he rang the doorbell.

seventeen

There's the bell. Right on time. Nori stopped to stare at herself in the entry mirror. She saw lipstick on her teeth, so she licked it off. Her eye shadow looked good, but then she'd had weeks to master the application. Cheeks. . .check. Hair. . . tolerable. Why was dressing up so traumatic?

Okay, she'd better get on with this. Nori opened the door.

Zachary looked at her and gasped.

Good response. Or not. Nori offered up her best smile.

"You look as pretty as an Easter egg," Zachary said.

Nori paused, trying to think how to respond.

Zachary blushed. "I didn't—"

"I'm sure you don't mean the oval part." Nori laughed.

"Not at all. You are color and light, and I don't think a woman could look more beautiful than you do right now."

Okay, now we're talking. "Thank you." Nori locked her door. "You look very handsome in that suit." Nori leaned toward him and touched the fabric. "Is that Italian?"

Zachary nodded. "Glad you like it."

Even though the date wasn't really a date, it felt like one to Nori. And to celebrate she decided not to recheck her door.

As they walked, her lavender dress made a swishing sound, her earrings swayed to the rhythm of their steps, and her perfume hovered in a delicate cloud. She knew the mood of the evening was suddenly becoming formal and datelike, but she also knew Lizza would want her to put aside her worries and enjoy it.

After a car ride up the hills and through a wooded area,

107

they pulled into the parking lot of Forrest Heights Chapel. Moments later, they entered a circular-shaped receiving area with marble floors, a glass ceiling, and a Greek statue in the middle. The crowd of guests milled around, chatting and generally looking elegant.

To their right, a man dressed in a tuxedo opened the French doors and led the crowd outside through the covered breezeway.

Nori glanced around. Lizza was nowhere in sight, but then she remembered that her friend was in the wedding party and was most likely busy attending the bride.

With his hand gently at her back, Zachary guided Nori through the breezeway. She noticed his palm felt solid and sure against her, and she relaxed at his touch.

When they arrived in the chapel, an usher offered Nori his arm, and they headed down the aisle with Zachary in their wake.

The building didn't appear to be a conventional church but a chapel built just for weddings and special occasions. Nori had always dreamed of a traditional wedding in the sanctuary of her own church, and yet she couldn't help but admire the splendor and elegance of Forrest Heights Chapel with its high cathedral ceilings and glass walls. So inspiring. And to have all the windows overlooking a natural forest as well as a waterfall created a mood of hushed reverence.

While they were being seated along with all the other guests, the organ began to play a majestic tune. Was it Bach? Then the family members were seated, each of the two mothers dressed in apricot gowns and the fathers dressed in black tuxedos.

Soon the flower girl, a cherub with dimples and red curls, marched down the aisle, dropping white rose petals from her little basket. Nori felt the usual tug on her spirit but reminded herself that families, the best as well as the worst, could fall apart without a moment's notice. Nori chided herself for her dark thoughts and turned her attention to the wedding party.

The first bridesmaid walked in and then the second and third. Each time, Nori looked for Lizza. Then with a flourish, the organ played the wedding march and everyone stood up. *Where is Lizza? Is she ill? Isn't she supposed to be a bridesmaid?*

The bride marched in, beaming with joy and wearing one of the loveliest dresses Nori had ever seen—an ivory satin gown embellished with a full-length cape made of delicate lace. Her hair was left long but adorned with a dazzling tiara. The whole effect was breathtaking.

Nori looked back and forth at the couple's faces. Their smiles radiated such love and promise that she was indeed moved. No doubt the devotion was real, and yet she couldn't help but wonder how those holy pledges started out so hopeful and ended up so desperate. Why couldn't couples stay together? Did people forget about their vows before the Almighty? Was marriage worth all the agony it could create?

Nori chewed on her lower lip. *Oh dear. I've become a cynic.* She tried once again to concentrate on the ceremony. The couple turned to face the front of the chapel, and the minister began to talk about joining their lives together as one. A few minutes later, the bride and groom began exchanging their vows.

Nori was determined not to cry, but mist filled her eyes anyway. Weddings always got to her, even now even amid the turmoil. She fumbled around in her purse for a tissue. Oh no. No tissue and her nose was running.

Without missing a beat, Zachary pulled a handkerchief from his pocket and handed it to her.

"Thank you," Nori mouthed. She dabbed her eyes and gently blew her nose. Then she listened again to the couple until all the lovely words were spent and all the promises made and the rings exchanged. Nori breathed a prayer for the couple, asking Him to give them both an extra measure of understanding and tender devotion toward each other and to guide and direct them all the days of their lives.

As the couple kissed, Nori suddenly recalled Lizza talking about her sister's curly blond hair. But the bride at the front of the chapel had long, wavy black hair. How could that be?

Oh no. Surely not.

Panic surged through Nori. Her mouth dropped open. She grabbed Zachary's arm. "I think we've attended the wrong wedding," she said in a hushed voice.

Zachary's surprise was tinged with a flicker of horror. "But how can it be the wrong wedding?" he whispered back.

Nori just shook her head and sunk a little lower in her seat. "I guess I zoned out when the minister said their names." *I've been crying over people I don't even know.*

After the song and a prayer, the minister introduced the couple as man and wife. They hurried down the aisle like they couldn't wait another second to start their lives together.

Guests rose to leave, but Nori stayed in her seat. She searched through her purse for the wedding invitation as Zachary looked on. Nori found the paper and scanned the words.

Zachary leaned over, looking at the invitation with her.

She pointed at the bottom line, which read: *Forrest Heights Chapel—The Rose Sanctuary.* "I can't believe I missed that last part, the Rose Sanctuary." Nori stared out into space. "It's all my fault. We went to the wrong wedding."

Zachary stared up at the front of the chapel and smiled. "But it was a good wedding."

Nori paused for a moment and then burst out laughing. "I guess it was." She looked around. Everyone else had gone.

"Oh my. Well, it's a good thing we didn't go to the wrong reception and dinner, too. It would have been a new level of embarrassment for me."

"That's usually *my* job," Zachary said.

"Why do you say that?" Nori leaned back in the pew.

"I don't think you really want to know."

"No, I do want to know." She glanced behind them. "There's nobody here but us."

Zachary looked at her as if to read her intentions. "Well, when I was growing up, awkwardness was so close to me it could have been a sibling. I guess you could say I was the odd rock in the pile."

Nori touched the padded seat near him. "How do you mean?"

"Well, anything that was different in school always stuck out. And *I* was different. I had the answers too quickly. My grades were too good. The teachers liked me too much. Somehow, that was objectionable. So I tried to hold back." He grinned. "Are you sure you want to hear this?"

Nori set her purse aside and turned toward him, wanting to make certain Zachary had her full attention. "I'm sure."

"Well, one time, when I was working on a science project, I realized it was going to be too technical, so I smashed the thing up and started over with an idea that was more. . . mediocre. I didn't want the grade as much as the approval. I tried to fit in, but it never worked. They'd already pegged me. It felt sort of like living in a suspended state. No one wanted Zachary, but no one would let him change." He fiddled with the button on his jacket. "Now I see how infantile that was, but back then, you couldn't have convinced me of it."

Nori remembered the kids in school being cruel at times, but she'd never spent time thinking about the sufferings of people who were brilliant. It seemed monstrously unfair to be ostracized for one's God-given abilities. "I'm so sorry that happened to you. That people couldn't just trust you with your gifts."

"Thanks. Was school ever hard on you?"

"Sometimes. I remember being very good at embarrassing myself. One time I tore my new clothes on a nail, and the accident exposed my undergarments to a whole gym full of kids." She shook her head. "That sort of thing seemed to happen to me more than the other girls for some reason. Anyway, after a while I began to assume that I'd embarrassed myself even when I hadn't. I'd find out later no one even noticed my blunder." She chuckled. "People are such strange collections of things. You know. . .all the miscellaneous hurts and fears we pick up along life's road. And then if we don't let go of anything, we find ourselves dragging all this stuff behind us."

"You, too?"

"Yeah. Me, too." She tugged on Zachary's jacket and grinned. After a bit more quiet had passed between them, Nori sighed. "Well, I guess we'd better go. We have a reception and dinner to attend. And hopefully, this time it'll be the *right* one."

They strode out of the chapel and back through the breezeway. When they arrived in the reception area, Nori noticed an archway with another sign that read THE ROSE SANCTUARY. She sighed. *Oh dear. Certainly too late now.* She just hoped Lizza wouldn't razz her too much about her faux pas.

Nori and Zachary headed down a hallway until they saw the opening to a banquet room. SILVERTON was displayed in front. "This is it. Lizza's sister married Anthony Silverton."

They gave each other a knowing smile and then chuckled in relief.

Zachary offered her his arm. "Shall we?"

She circled her arm through his, and they strolled into the banquet room. The word *splendiferous* came to mind. Crystal chandeliers dazzled the room, and gilded trim adorned all the wainscoting and chairs. Fine linen covered the tables, and white birdcages brimming with yellow roses served as romantic centerpieces. The bride had truly created a fairy-tale scene.

Nori raised her chin. She refused to let such a blissful evening be tainted with her own musings, so she guarded her heart as best she could. She busied herself, trying to spot Lizza somewhere in the crowd. She was certain they'd made it into the right reception, but she still didn't see her friend among the clusters of guests. Perhaps she was off mingling in another room or powdering her nose.

Zachary motioned toward the atrium. "Looks like they have hors d'oeuvres and something to drink in there. Are you thirsty?"

"I am."

Once again, being the perfect gentleman, Zachary touched the small of her back and gently steered her through the crowd, through the wafting mandolin music, and into the atrium. Nori ordered sparkling mineral water with lime, and Zachary requested a root beer with extra ice.

When they were situated with their drinks, they walked over to the fountain and watched the water as it flowed and sparkled down five tiers. The water continued its descent, narrowing into a stream and then collecting in a small pool, which was nestled in a tropical garden.

"How lovely," Nori said.

Zachary stared at the sight. "*Lovely* is a subjective term."

"Oh, is it?"

He released a grin. "Yes, it can be subject to opinion, false speculation, and irrational emotions."

Nori lifted an eyebrow, deciding to rise to the occasion. "So in your opinion, which is of course riddled with emotion and speculation, would you say that the fountain and garden are lovely?"

He stared at it. "They have their benefits."

"And what are those?" She batted her eyelids.

"They please you. And that's enough for me."

"That's nice, but don't you want something for yourself?" Nori asked.

Zachary looked at her. "I do indeed."

eighteen

Nori felt her face flush, wishing she hadn't asked the question quite that way. The moment had become unexpectedly intimate. But on the other hand, she wasn't about to shy away from it. She glanced his way again. There was something different about his expression— perhaps an understanding had grown between them.

She took a sip of her drink as she pondered the lives of married folks who'd made it to their golden years—the couples whose love was tethered so closely that it could not be undone. She guessed they died with a sweetness on their brow, knowing what it was like to be truly cared for. And truly known. Faithful love did exist; she knew that—and yet reservations persisted. But what could she do with these new feelings for Zachary except follow her heart just a little?

With a murmur and a nod between them, Nori and Zachary strolled over to a more secluded spot—a glassed-in alcove, which gave them a spectacular view of the heavens

Nori loved the way the stars decorated the night sky, like cut crystals shimmering in a box of black velvet.

They sat down together on a wooden settee near the windows. "Ever since I was a little girl, I've been planning a wedding. My own wedding," Nori said without thinking. Perhaps she shouldn't reveal such intimate details to him. But she was in the mood to take a chance.

Zachary's eyes lit up with what looked like surprise. Or panic. "Really?" He took a sip of his beverage and then set it down on a small table.

"It's true."

He leaned closer to her. "I wish I'd been one of your friends back then. You know, maybe one of your neighbors. We could have played together, and I could have given your bridal dolls a ride on my Starship Enterprise."

Nori laughed. *Okay, this guy is sorta funny, too. So glad he wasn't upset with my revelation.*

"I hope what's happened to your parents hasn't wiped out all your dreams."

She thought for a moment. "They could never take away all my dreams."

Zachary nodded. "So, what was your ideal wedding? You know. . .when you did all that planning, you must have come up with something spectacular."

"I don't think you. . .I mean, guys don't usually want to hear about all the froufrou details—"

Zachary covered her hands with his and squeezed. "I do. . . want to hear it. All of it."

"Okay." Nori looked down at their hands.

Zachary released her.

A tingling sensation ran through Nori, starting with her fingers and racing all across her skin. "Sorry, what was I talking about?" She tried to gather her thoughts, but she felt distracted.

"Your dream wedding."

"Oh yes. Actually, I haven't thought about it in a while. Let's see. My colors were emerald and ivory for a winter wedding. Lots of greenery with ivory satin ribbons. Having more greenery than flowers would save money, but it would also look very elegant. And there'd be clusters of ivory candles, more than anyone could count. An organ for "The Wedding March," but a harpist to accompany one specially chosen song." Her hands closed together. "And a gown of Victorian lace with a scandalously long train."

"Sounds very nice. And what about the groom?"

Nori glanced away. "Well, I suppose a black tux is always stylish." She looked back at him. He wore an unreadable expression. The truth was, when she played wedding as a child, the groom part seemed too fanciful. Even as a young woman, she'd always had a hard time imagining anyone proposing to her. Maybe she should steer the topic onto a safer road. "I even used to bake little wedding cakes. Of course, my first ones were always made of mud."

Zachary chuckled.

His laugh made her grow warm inside. Nori noticed that Zachary's awkwardness and hesitancy were almost gone. Perhaps she'd made him more comfortable around women. Maybe he just needed some practice. In other words, he needed a female friend. But the stirring inside her didn't feel like mere friendship.

She studied Zachary's face. In the beginning, she had indeed misunderstood who he was. There was so much to discover about him—things that had to be quietly sought. Before she could censor herself, Nori spoke from her heart. "Zachary, I said I just wanted us to be friends. . .and that this evening was not a date. . ." She looked at him. "But I've changed my mind. Would that be all right with you?"

&

Zachary blinked a few times to make sure he was conscious. He could hardly believe what Nori had just said. "It's what I've prayed for all day."

Nori reached up and touched his cheek.

When she released him, he caught her hand and kissed it. *Oh wow.* That was pretty risky. They'd only made the date official by about five seconds, and he was already kissing her hand. Although he certainly wanted to do that weeks ago.

Months ago. "So, if this is a date, do you mind if I ask you something. . .personal?" Zachary knew he might lose every inch he'd gained by continuing, but he had to have an answer to his query.

"I guess so."

"If you ever do follow through with your dream wedding, what *kind* of groom are you looking for?"

Nori went quiet for a moment. Extra quiet. Long enough, in fact, that he hoped he hadn't embarrassed her with such a delicate topic.

"Well," she finally began, "I would want to marry a kind and faithful Christian. Beyond that, maybe someone who's smart and funny, too." Nori looked away, fingering her evening dress.

Zachary thought those were all good qualities, but he wasn't really sure how Nori perceived him, except that she was with him now and she wanted more than friendship between them. He'd take that for a good sign.

"And what are you looking for. . .in a spouse?"

Zachary wanted to reply, "I've found the one I'm looking for," but he decided to say, "I'm looking for the same qualities you are."

He caught Nori with that faraway gaze again. The same way she looked when she talked about her perfect wedding day. Wistful, with childlike wonder. Happy. And utterly beautiful.

"By the way," he asked, "do you like dreams?"

"I like the good ones."

"Yes, well, last night I dreamed about you," Zachary said.

"You did? Tell me about it. . .that is, if it's good." Nori leaned toward him.

Zachary felt himself stepping into unfamiliar territory. Well, more like leaping into unknown waters without a boat or life jacket. Or the ability to swim. But with Nori, he couldn't help himself. "I dreamed I'd been dropped into a tunnel, dark and cold. I stumbled along for what seemed like days, and then just when I thought I might never escape, I turned a corner and saw a soft yellow light. Slowly the illumination morphed into something else."

"What was it?" Nori eyes widened.

"You. You were the warm light I'd been searching for."

"Oh my." A tiny gasp escaped Nori's lips.

"Is something wrong?"

"No, nothing's wrong. Except. . .I've had the same dream about you."

"Oh?" Zachary stroked his finger against his lip, thinking about divine assistance.

"How strange is that? I mean, this can't be. Can it? To have us both dream the same thing?" Nori gazed up at the stars and then back at him.

"I like to figure out things. I'm pretty good at it. But there are some things in this life, even with the help of science, that defy our understanding. Some things must be left to mystery. Such as the size of the universe, splitting atoms. . .love."

"So are you happy just to leave mysteries unsolved?" Nori asked.

Zachary raised his chin and spread out his hands in an attempt to be dramatic. "If there isn't enough data at the time to make a clear hypothesis, then what else is there but conjecture. . .or to revel in the unknown?"

Nori chuckled. "I suppose so."

He'd gone this far, so Zachary decided to take one more dangerous step. "Would you go out with me tomorrow evening?"

Nori gave him one of those pauses again—the kind that made him sweat.

"All right," she finally said. "What will we do?"

"Well, I thought you could come over to my apartment and I could make us some supper."

Nori pulled back, looking shocked. "You mean you actually bake things and fry things and roast things?"

He nodded. "I grill, too."

She cocked her head. "Are you sure you're not just trying to trick me into coming over to cook for you?"

"Never." Zachary placed his hand over his heart. "I like to cook. I love it, in fact. I could make salmon with rosemary, Caesar salad, and chocolate mousse for dessert. Anyway, after I feed you, I thought we could settle in front of my big-screen TV. There's going to be a *Star Trek* marathon." Was that another grimace? *Oh, that last suggestion might have come off a bit peculiar.* Or was she upset about the salmon? Maybe women hated fish. "Or I could make you stuffed pork chops or filet mignon. . .whatever you'd like."

"Oh no, that's fine," Nori said. "I love fish. I just find it shocking that you cook. Do you want me to bring anything?"

He shook his head. "Just you. That's all I want." His face heated up. "Six thirty?"

Nori curled a strand of blond hair around her finger. "Yes, six thirty is perfect."

⁂

After congratulating the newly married couple and enjoying the wedding dinner to the fullest, Zachary deposited Nori at her door. He'd hoped to give her a good night kiss, but the moment didn't feel quite right. Their first kiss shouldn't be rushed or taken lightly. He knew little about women, but for some reason, on that one point, he felt certain. And then he remembered his prayer about not wanting to get ahead of the Lord. Yes, he would celebrate the romancing of Nori Kelly, but he would also let it unfold in a way that would please God.

Then Zachary did the only thing he could think to do

before entertaining the love of his life—he microcleaned his apartment. He made certain the kitchen was sanitized and the bathroom was devoid of anything embarrassing.

At 1:00 a.m., exhausted from cleaning, Zachary fell into bed with all his clothes on. He stared up at the ceiling, knowing he was way too restless and wired to sleep. So he allowed his mind to focus on the wedding reception and dinner. *What an evening.* It'd turned out much better than he'd ever imagined.

He drummed his fingers on the sheet. *However,* when he'd dropped Nori off at her door, she'd paused, looking at him with a curious smile. Had she been waiting for a kiss? What would he do when the time *was* right? He couldn't think of anything finer than kissing Nori Kelly, but he'd never kissed a woman before. And he wasn't sure what to do. He'd watched couples kissing in movies, yet the process looked problematic. So much could go wrong. Too many variables. Where did one put one's hands? And then there was the matter of how much pressure to the lips. How long should a kiss last? And what did people say after a kiss? Were there secrets he was unaware of?

Zachary punched his pillow. How peculiar. He could manage twenty geophysical applications, but he couldn't manage a simple kiss. He'd probably end up slobbering all over Nori or saying something stupid, and she'd slam the door in his face.

The image of her being upset with him and banging the door in his face wouldn't play out in his head. She wouldn't be so rude, but she might disappear from his life. He could imagine that easily enough.

He hurled his shoes through his open closet door and then bounced on his pillow a few times. But all inclinations toward drowsiness eluded him. And he knew well what pebble of worry was rubbing his thoughts raw. *The wedding date had simply been too easy.* They'd floated around in an evening made perfect by a beautiful setting and expensive food. The environment was so splendid, Nori would have been happy next to a block of wood. But his apartment date would be an ordinary evening. *It will be a test.* He knew where he stood concerning his feelings for Nori, but if she didn't enjoy a regular evening in his apartment, how would he expect her to spend the rest of her life with him?

Zachary jammed his pillow over his head. Maybe his thinking was way off. In his mind, he was treating Nori like a pet he wanted to pamper and please so she wouldn't run off. But that wasn't how love worked. Was it?

He was fairly certain his parents' divorce had tainted his views on matrimony, and yet he still believed God could make a marriage last a lifetime. But first things first. He'd only had one date with Nori, and there was no acknowledgment or hint of love. Just the hope of it.

Maybe he'd better go clean the bathroom. One more time.

nineteen

The next day, when the hour of Nori's arrival approached, Zachary nearly lost his cool. He opened the oven door again and poked at the salmon with a fork to make sure it wasn't overcooked. Then he put on some jazz music and dimmed the bright lights.

Zachary checked the bathroom for the tenth time and realized his obsessive-compulsive disorder had reached an all-time high. "Calm down," he kept chanting to himself. *Do other men act like this?* He doubted it. Only nerds with compulsive behavior.

He groaned as he fingered his hair. *Oh no.* He'd slathered on too much gel. The strands had glued together, giving his hair the suppleness of molded plastic.

Trying to figure out how to de-gel his hair, Zachary focused on the problem by rubbing his finger back and forth over his upper lip. *Oh no.* Stubble. He glanced in the entry mirror. He'd forgotten to shave. How in the world could that have happened?

Was he losing his mind over a girl? "I believe I am," he said. Well, at least his khakis were new and his shirt was as crisp as celery.

The doorbell rang, and all fidgeting ceased. He walked to the door, and on opening it, he found Nori smiling, dressed casually, and looking ready for a good evening. And to her credit she said nothing about his plastered hair or five o'clock shadow.

Maybe all his intense worry was unnecessary. "Hi there." Nori's face radiated warmth.

Zachary felt mesmerized by her presence and pondered how easy it would be to gaze upon her face for a lifetime. Maybe he should stop gaping and say something. "Would you like to come in?"

Nori stepped over the threshold and into his abode. She looked around the room, appearing to study each object on his wall.

I guess stuff on display was always the litmus test. Very telling. Earlier when she'd been in his apartment, Nori had been so distraught about her parents that she hadn't gotten so up close and personal with his wall displays. He found himself holding his breath as she stared at his accomplishments.

"My, my. You were chess champion in college? And president of the math club. And a magna cum laude graduate. And valedictorian. Look at all these awards. And now geophysicist of the year. This is incredible." She touched the award on the table and then looked at him. "You are one impressive man."

Zachary wanted to smile. No, he really wanted to do an arm pump and cheer. Or maybe laugh like a cage full of hyenas—but he just bit his lip instead and said, "Thanks."

Nori continued to look at all his memorabilia like it mattered—like she was making an effort to get to know him, understand him. After she'd asked about everything on the wall as well as the table, she slid her hands into the pockets of her pants.

Guess she was waiting for an invitation to sit down. Or was he supposed to offer her something to drink? "Are you hungry?" *Food. Oh no.* "I smell something burning." *The salmon!* Zachary ran to the kitchen and yanked the oven door open. Smoked poured out. He waved, coughed a few times, and then stared in horror at the sight. His salmon was not only overcooked, it'd become a fish-shaped cinder block.

Nori rushed in, grabbed the oven mitts, and pulled out the baking dish of sizzling salmon.

"Thanks," Zachary said. "I got kinda paralyzed just looking at it."

Nori stared into the baking dish and then poked at it with a fork. "You know, I think it's going to be okay. We'll just eat the middle part."

He sighed at the fish. The tree-like sprigs of fresh rosemary, which had been gingerly placed on top of the fish, now looked like the charred remains of a forest fire. "But the whole thing will taste burnt."

"Maybe not." Nori found a spatula in the drawer. "Let's hurry up and get it out of this pan."

They worked together for a few minutes to salvage whatever they could and placed a few chunks of salmon on their two plates.

He shook his head, staring at the mess. *Yep, dead, burned slabs of fish.* "I'm sorry. It's not edible."

"I'm the one who should be apologizing. I kept you in the living room too long. I should have asked you if I could help you in the kitchen."

How gracious was that? Zachary smiled at her. "It's okay." He turned his attention to the empty table and reached for salads and dressing, warm bread, homemade tartar sauce for the salmon, olives, cottage cheese, and anything else he could think of that would make his culinary disaster look a little less. . .well, disastrous.

When they finally sat down to eat, Zachary felt a lengthy but sincere prayer coming on, which he said out loud, asking God to not only bless the food to the nourishment of their bodies but to help it go down okay. Then he added a secret prayer that Nori wouldn't run away the moment the dinner was over.

Zachary watched Nori take her first bite of salmon. His leg bounced under the table as he waited for her response.

"It's good," she said. "It doesn't taste burned at all." Then she dug into the rest of the meal, making positive comments about the homemade bread and the salad.

He finally relaxed enough to eat. When they'd finished, Zachary rose to get the mousse from the fridge. He set one of the goblets in front of Nori.

"You made mousse? For me?"

Zachary nodded. "It's not too hard to make." He tried not to stare and chuckle as Nori raved and moaned over every bite of dessert. *Guess she likes it.*

Nori leaned her dessert goblet over and scraped out the last bite of mousse. "Well, now *that* was inspiring." She rested back in her chair. "I've never known a guy who liked to cook. Ever."

"Cooking is relaxing. Well, when I'm not burning things."

Nori chuckled.

"It makes me think about something besides work." Zachary picked up his dishes and set them in the sink.

Nori gathered her dishes together and followed him to the counter.

When he turned around, she was so close he almost started.

"You have a little mousse on the corner of your mouth." She reached up with her napkin and gently touched his face.

Zachary noticed that she had the same dreamy expression she'd worn the previous evening when he'd said good night. What should he do?

A lengthy pause ensued.

Should I take a chance and kiss her? He wondered what his odds were of success—probably 60/40 in his favor. But then again. . .

Before Zachary could go through an entire protracted debate in his head, Nori laced her fingers at the back of his neck and kissed him full on the mouth.

Oh, dearest, sweet Nori. Her lips—soft, moist, and inviting. If he'd known kissing Nori was going to be such rapture, the wait would have been agony. But now the wait was over, and so were his fears. He cupped her face in his hands and kissed her, hoping she could feel every bit of the love in his heart.

After a good long kiss, Nori pulled back, looked into his eyes, and then kissed his temples, cheeks, and chin.

Zachary closed his eyes to enjoy the full effect of her touch. Could life get any finer?

She placed her fingers over his mouth. "You have such wonderful lips. I never knew."

He chuckled and kissed the fingers that touched his lips. Zachary then slipped one hand around her waist and pulled her closer for another round of kissing. He wondered why he'd ever been so timid about kissing Nori. It was the most natural thing in the world. Natural and normal and yet extraordinary in every way. He felt as if he'd waited his whole life for this moment. He was home. Right here and now. With Nori in his arms.

When they let the kiss come to a tender close, Nori chuckled. "You know, I'd been wondering what it would be like to kiss you."

"Now you know," Zachary said. "And how was it?"

"Oh, I can assure you, it was all that it needed to be." Nori smiled. "And more."

"Well, I'm *very* glad for that."

"And what did you think?"

He looked at her. "You really want to know?"

"I do."

Zachary cleared his throat. "I think your kiss packs enough energy to cause a solar flare and enough celestial wonder to make an atheist believe in God."

Nori's mouth eased open, and her face lit up. "What an incredible compliment. I. . .uh. . .well, you've left me astonished." She released a nervous chuckle.

Even though Zachary would have loved to continue discussing the euphoria of her kiss, he suddenly felt self-conscious at his own frankness and fervor. "So, did you get plenty of supper?"

She paused, gazing at him. "Yes, thank you. It was *all* wonderful." Then Nori leaned over the sink and started to rinse off one of the plates.

Zachary lifted the dish from her hands. "You shouldn't have to do that."

"But I don't mind. In fact, when I fix you dinner, I'll make you help clean up." She winked.

"All right." He was so pleased to hear her talk of their future plans together that he couldn't refuse her. It was a good thing he made a fine income, because he knew he'd never be able to deny her anything.

They worked side by side, and when the cleanup was done and the dishwasher was softly humming, they headed to the living room.

Zachary pushed a button, and a large flat-paneled television rose up out of a mahogany cabinet.

"Oh. I've never seen a TV rise up out of nowhere before." Nori snuggled down on the couch like a bird in a nest. "Nice."

"You know, we don't *have* to watch science fiction. I also like other kinds of movies."

"Oh yeah?" Nori rested her chin in her palm. "Like what?"

"Well, I have one chick flick." Zachary pulled out a DVD and blew off so much dust that he coughed.

She grinned. "Only one?"

Zachary knew he looked a little sheepish. "Well, the truth is I ordered a sci-fi film, and they sent me this by accident."

twenty

The evening with Zachary played itself out more beautifully than Nori could have ever imagined, and too soon, she thought, they were strolling back to her front door. "I had a great time," she said.

Zachary looked away for a second and then grinned at her. "You mean even with salmon that was burned beyond recognition?"

"Well, I'd say it was more fashionably *blackened*."

He chuckled.

When they arrived at her apartment, Nori wondered— hoped, in fact—that Zachary would kiss her good night.

After a moment of quiet expectation, Zachary moved closer to her. Instead of kissing her, he reached out and cupped her face in his hand. And then he let his fingers brush lightly across her cheek.

Nori closed her eyes, absorbing the warm and tender sensation of his touch. She couldn't help but notice the way he handled her—as if she were made of the most delicate china.

Ahh, no more princess of the friendship date. No more desperate times and desperate measures. And no more kissing the mirror!

Zachary continued to explore the contours of her face. "You are so beautiful in every way," he whispered in her ear.

How long had she dreamed of a man who would care about her like this? It seemed like forever. And now Zachary was here. He'd been so near, yet she'd never seen him. How could that be? *Well, I certainly see him now.* Just as she was about to open her eyes, Nori could feel his lips against hers.

After a tender kiss, Zachary eased away. "Boy, this makes geophysical interpretations seem *sooo* dull."

Nori laughed. "You're funny."

"I am?"

"The things you say. You're so honest and kind."

"That doesn't sound very funny *or* romantic."

She placed her hand over her heart. "Oh, it is to *me*."

Moments later, after a few more merry good nights, Nori closed the door and readied herself for bed. She realized that in weeks, even hours really, her impressions of Zachary had changed into something totally different. She found him to be not only smart but loving and thoughtful and even funny in a sweet sort of way. And the biggest surprise of all was the gradual attraction she felt.

Gradual. She laughed. There wasn't anything gradual about the way she felt when Zachary first kissed her. Then Nori remembered that she'd kissed Zachary first. She was a little embarrassed about that. But not *too* embarrassed. She could tell he'd wanted to kiss her. Why he'd hesitated before she had no idea, but he wasn't faltering anymore.

Nori climbed under her comforter and scooted between the cotton sheets. She let their cooling softness soothe her wide-eyed emotions, and yet something untouched lingered in her spirit. Feeling too tired to explore all the emotions of the day, she snuggled into the pillow and closed her eyes, hoping for sleep.

Imaginings, light and airy, came to her like dangling willow branches swaying and dipping in the breeze. The little zephyr in her thoughts lifted her away into another world. She no longer had the will to hold onto her consciousness, so she released it like a kite on a wind-filled day.

Nori saw herself running in a field of golden clover. She had no idea how long she'd been there, but it felt like a lifetime. All was lovely and free and lit with sun. Happiness reigned in that place, and all was at peace.

Without warning, the autumn fields withered before her eyes and everything, all the flowers and bees and grasses, became laden with a gray wintry frost. Darkness spread over the fields, and an unseen oppression weighed heavily on her chest. Winds, biting and cold, lashed against her face until she could no longer breathe. A scream caught in her throat.

Then a hand, warm and strong, reached out to her, pulling her away from the peril. In one sweeping gesture, the fields of light were restored. She was home.

But in the midst of paradise revisited, she felt alone for the first time. But why? Who was her rescuer? Her hero? His face was in a shadow, his sweetness hidden from her. And yet she felt a familiarity when she'd touched his hand.

"Don't go," she heard someone say. "You must not go. Your time here isn't over."

Was she dreaming or living? She must find out the man's name and why he'd come.

Zachary.

Nori stirred out of a deep sleep, her heart racing and her body moist with perspiration. She rose up in bed, tossed back the covers, and looked around the room. The dream seemed so real. Too real.

Nori touched her palm and fingers where she'd felt his hand in hers. She knew her mind was playing tricks on her, but she could still felt the warmth of his touch. In spite of her flustered and whirling thoughts, the true meaning of the dream soon became realized.

I'm falling in love.

"How can this be?" Nori's heart made a few more hard and

scary pounds before she calmed herself. *I'm still in control here.* She could take their relationship as slowly as she wanted to. He would wait for her. Wouldn't he?

She thought of Zachary and wondered what he was doing right now. Was he researching on the Internet? Making more chocolate mousse? Or was he also punching his pillow, curious as to why two ordinary dates had become like a surprise attack. Maybe he was scared and wary, too. Maybe that's why he had always hesitated in kissing her. He didn't want to get in too deep. Or too lost in love.

Too lost in love. She repeated the words out loud, listening to the sound of them. The word *lost* did seem appropriate since the feeling of losing one's heart to someone felt like being lost in a dark forest with no hope of light or rescue. She was lost in love, and there was no way out. But did she need a way out? Probably. Most likely. *I don't know.* But couldn't even the sweetest love eventually dissolve like melting snow?

She tried to fall asleep again, but thoughts of her parents plagued her. If they weren't getting a divorce all would look differently. She wouldn't be ruled by fear. But how could she fear what was so good and kind? With that thought, Nori let herself sink back into sleep.

❧

Monday morning came softly, even though she'd tossed and turned all night. Nori rose, rubbing her back. She needed a new mattress. A new nightgown. And a new point of view. And she definitely needed some prayer. "Oh, Lord, please help my parents to seek You first in all their decisions, and please help me not to be so injured from their choices that I miss Your will for my life."

Nori looked through the night-table drawer for her Bible but couldn't find it. Had she misplaced it? She made a quick search through the apartment and finally found a copy in her closet.

How sad and sorry was that? It had obviously been too long.

She sat on the loveseat in her bedroom and let her Bible fall open to her all-time favorite chapter, Psalm 121. *"I lift up my eyes to the hills—where does my help come from? My help comes from the LORD, the Maker of heaven and earth. He will not let your foot slip—he who watches over you will not slumber. . . ."*

How could she have forgotten some of God's most basic and loving promises? How could she have let that knowledge slip away from her heart even for a moment? She read further down into the chapter: *"The sun will not harm you by day, nor the moon by night. The LORD will keep you from all harm—he will watch over your life; the LORD will watch over your coming and going both now and forevermore."*

Could any scripture be more beautiful or comforting? It was hard to truly fathom His love and care.

He is watching me even now. He would take care of her needs. Every bit of confusion and fear and doubt. She embraced the book and thanked God for His Word.

Nori remembered how God used dreams to speak to people in the Bible and wondered if He was giving her guidance through her dreams about Zachary. Could God still speak to people while they were sleeping? He was God, and He was still in the business of miracles. All things were possible with the Lord. That she believed, too.

Placing the Bible on the top of her nightstand, she made a vow to herself and to God to reach out to His word daily, not just when it was convenient or when she found herself in a tough situation.

Peace didn't flood over Nori, but she did feel a trickle. And it felt good. She decided to continue dating Zachary, but she would take her time—fall in love at her own pace. Of course at that speed, it might take years, but she was sure Zachary would wait.

❧

Nori went through her usual morning routine—locked her door, checked it, and then headed to the elevator on her way to Sweet Nothings.

Zachary met her. They stood in the hallway mesmerized by each other for a moment. He reached out and touched her cheek.

The gesture felt so intimate that Nori felt her cheeks heat up. "Hi."

Ivan Wentworth emerged from his apartment.

Zachary and Nori grinned at each other as they joined Ivan in his trek toward the elevator.

Ivan looked back at her. "Nori?"

"Yes?" She caught up with Ivan but wondered what he could want. He was usually too enamored with his techno gadgets to notice her.

"I was just wondering if you'd like to go out to dinner sometime." Ivan slipped his PDA into his pocket and gave her his attention.

Zachary let out a puff of air that sounded like disgust.

Nori couldn't believe a neighbor would ask her out in front of Zachary—as if he were invisible. "I'm sorry, Ivan, but I guess I'll pass."

Ivan blinked a few times. "Really?"

They all three stepped into the elevator. The doors closed like a tomb, sealing them in together.

After Nori mashed the "G" button several times, silence seeped in, filling the small space like a suffocating, tar-like smoke. Nori wanted to cough but swallowed instead.

twenty-one

Nori kept her eyes straight ahead, since she was too afraid to look Zachary in the eye.

"May I ask you why?" Ivan sounded hurt.

She winced, wishing she were somewhere else. Anywhere else. Like maybe in a den of hungry wolverines. How much should she say to Ivan? "I appreciate the invitation. But I'm dating Zachary right now." *Oh no.* How did that come out of her mouth? *Way too much information, Nori.* She should have stuck with "No."

Ivan glanced over at his competition and winced. "Oh, I see."

Nori was proud of Zachary. He'd crossed his arms in irritation, but he'd remained silent.

Ivan slapped the ground floor button like it was a mosquito. "There's something wrong with this elevator." When the doors suddenly opened, Ivan escaped with a weak smile and a wave.

Zachary held the door for Nori. "You okay?"

"Yes."

"So, I guess from the sounds of the conversation. . .we're involved." Zachary's expression told her he was more pleased than surprised with her admission.

"I do believe we are." Uncertainty and hesitation still lingered in her heart, but the moment called for a smile, and so she gave him one. A good one.

"I'm glad you feel that way." Zachary's voice held a cheerful lilt.

"But. . .I just don't know how much yet. I hope that's okay."

"I understand." He looked at her. "I'll see you later."

"I certainly hope so." Nori gave him a little salute good-bye. As she drove to work, her thoughts settled on to the shop.

The second she entered the glass doors at Sweet Nothings, Lizza was all over her with questions. "So what happened with Zachary at the wedding? We've barely had a chance to talk. Come on, tell me everything. Please. Please."

Nori put up her hands. "Okay, I surrender." She smiled. "Well, we ate. By the way, the filet mignon was the best I've ever had. Cooked to perfection. And that baked Alaska for dessert? What a unique idea. You're—"

"Yeah, the food was incredible. But what about you and Zachary?"

"Well, we talked, and we—"

"You know what I mean. I want the juicy parts. Come on. You gotta give 'em up."

"Zachary and I had a nice time," Nori singsonged as she walked around the shop looking for things to do. *I suppose she does deserve a few details, since she helped orchestrate the whole thing.*

Lizza gestured to keep going. "And?"

Nori wasn't sure how much to say. She decided to toss out one more point of interest. "We're dating, and—"

"I knew it. We have a touchdown." Lizza's arms shot up as she made crowd noises.

Nori laughed at her friend. "I'm taking my time."

"Girl, you're light-years beyond that."

"And how do you know?"

"Because I see something in your eyes." Lizza tilted her head and narrowed her eyes. "Something that wasn't there before."

"Probably just dust off one of the shelves."

"Hey, these shelves aren't dusty, and you know it." Lizza

crossed her arms. "You've got a twinkle in your eye."

"A twinkle?"

"Yeah, you know, a sparkle, a glimmer of something that wasn't there before. You have the glow when a woman is falling. . ."

"Falling?" Nori asked.

"Yes, falling."

"It's probably more like bending a little."

"Sure it is." Lizza shook her head.

"Who can know love? For certain, I mean."

"Listen, love is a freight train. When you're hit, you know it."

Nori chuckled. "Well, what if it's a toy train?"

Her friend just sighed at her as she hid the feather duster and paper towels under the counter.

"I guess I'll mop the floor before the customers get here," Nori said.

"I already mopped the floor this morning."

"You're the best." Nori patted Lizza on the back and then headed to the cash register. "You're not a good shrink, but you're the best in every other way."

Lizza followed Nori. "I'm not giving up that easily. Not very long ago, you were so ready to fall in love. I know what's happening to your parents is bothering you."

Nori took in a deep breath, wishing Lizza would let it go. She wasn't in the mood to talk about her parents. "I won't deny it."

"Did your dad ever return your messages?"

"No."

"Boy, that's tough."

"He's not trying to be mean," Nori said. "Although that's the way it feels. He's just trying to avoid my lectures."

"And would you lecture him?"

Nori thought for a moment. "Well, it wouldn't start out

that way. But sooner or later I know I'd want to ask a few pointed questions."

"But still, your dad should call you so you can deal with it."

"I've been *dealing* with it for weeks." Nori rearranged some jars of stick candy on the counter. And then rearranged them again.

"But have you? I mean, I know you've said you're obsessed about their divorce. But that's not the same as *dealing* with it."

Nori tried not to overreact. She felt like getting angry, but she got quiet instead. She didn't like having her remarks thrown back in her face, especially when she'd said them in a vulnerable moment. In fact, she would like to have told Lizza to mind her own business. But Lizza was a friend as well as an employee, and since they'd allowed each other certain inroads into each other's lives, it was indeed Lizza's business. "I don't know. You might be right."

"I wish you could talk to your parents. Maybe it would give you some closure. You know, so this doesn't ruin your life." Lizza placed a hand on Nori's shoulder. "I just hate to see *their* decision cause you to miss out on the joy you were meant to have."

Lizza's words were soft but piercing, too. *She's right.* "I know it takes a lot of courage to talk to friends candidly. I appreciate that." And then with that statement, Nori hoped the conversation had come to a close.

"Well, you know what else would help?"

Oh no. Not more advice.

Lizza wiggled her eyebrows. "Some of these buttercream truffles we got yesterday." She pulled a silvery box out from under the counter, opened the lid, and breathed in the fragrance. "Oh, I never tire of all these free samples."

"Yeah, that's because you have a waistline." Nori groaned.

"You do, too. You've lost a bunch of weight."

"Well, mainly because—" Their banter was interrupted by the bell over the door.

Zachary walked in the shop, his shoulders sagging and his expression twisted in pain.

They all said their hellos and then Nori strode over to him, alarmed. "What's the matter?" She hoped something terrible hadn't happened.

"This probably isn't the best time, but I felt you should know right away," Zachary said.

"Please tell me what's happening." Nori touched his arm.

"I'm being asked to move to Denver. Immediately." Zachary looked away. When he looked back at her, his eyes were misty.

twenty-two

"Denver?" Nori released Zachary's arm. "But why?"

"My boss just informed me that South Gate is moving its operations there. Everybody goes to Colorado, or we lose our jobs." Zachary thought this had to be the worst day of his life. Just when he'd formed a genuine connection with Nori. They'd have to try to develop a long-distance relationship. He'd rarely seen that option work among his coworkers, since the detachment usually meant a breakdown of the resolve to stay close.

"Denver is pretty far away." Nori's voice sounded bewildered.

"Yes, it is." Zachary knew one alternative that would solve their problems. Marriage. But that answer created new problems. Nori's business was successful, and he was pretty certain she'd never want to move. Nor could he ever ask her to make that sacrifice. "I could quit my job," he said.

"Do you have other job prospects here?"

He shook his head. "I wish I did. This isn't a big oil town, so there aren't that many opportunities. If I quit my job, I'm not certain I'll get another one here." Zachary realized his new plan wasn't going to fly the minute he'd thought it. How could he ask her to marry him if he had no job? He certainly wasn't going to let Nori marry a loafer.

"You can't quit your job." Nori shook her head. "I don't want you to."

From the back of the shop, Lizza cleared her throat. "I have everything under control. Nori, you go on with Zachary. You guys look like you need a minute."

"Good idea," he said. "Do you want to go for a walk?"

"Some fresh air. Maybe that will help us think more clearly."

Well, at least she was saying "us." That was a good sign. Zachary opened the door for her, and they strolled down the sidewalk toward their favorite spot—Arlington Lawn at The Promenade. Once they'd climbed the stairs and they were seated by the mist, Zachary took Nori's hand. It was time for some honesty. Some revelations. "I care about you, Nori. A great deal."

"I care about you, too," she said.

Zachary gazed at her. The surrounding light made Nori's eyes look like the color of the sea. But something else shone in her eyes. He hoped it might be love. Now that they'd shared some of their feelings, he couldn't imagine himself saying good-bye, even if they promised to build a long-distance relationship.

If he did propose to her, she would at least discover the extent of his feelings. Then maybe God would take care of the rest. Somehow He could work everything out. Did he have that much blind faith? He breathed in. "It's more than just caring. I love you. I have for a long time. . .from afar, I guess you could say."

"You love me?" Nori sounded confused, maybe even a little scared.

"Yes." Zachary looked around, grateful the park had emptied of visitors. At least for the moment. But the clouds above them had darkened, and he hoped they wouldn't be interrupted by a storm. With resolve and a feeling of urgency, he scooted off the bench and knelt on one knee. "Nori Kelly, would you do me the honor of becoming my wife?"

"Be your wife?" Nori looked down at their fingers, which were intertwined. "But we barely know each other. I don't mean to belittle what you've said. It's a generous and lovely offer, and I'm grateful. But. . ."

This isn't going well. Zachary tried not to panic.

Nori slipped her hand from his. "Except for the times we've spent together recently, we've only had bits of conversations outside our apartments."

He rose to his feet. "Love isn't subject to time. . .or anything else."

"I thought maybe we should date for a few months. To see if what we felt would grow. It's too soon." Nori stepped over to the cascades and looked over the edge.

Zachary sat down for a moment, begging God for some help and hoping Nori would come back to the bench. But she didn't come back.

He walked over to her and looked down at the steam coming off the rocks. Perhaps he'd gotten ahead of God. Once again. *Well, that feels familiar.*

He stood in silence next to Nori as he stared out over the battered rocks. The ever-rising water vapor always reminded him of something celestial—perhaps angels sweeping about, only half materializing. He wondered how Nori saw the mist. More importantly, he wondered what she was thinking about right now. What he wouldn't give to know all her thoughts—to be able to overcome all her fears by saying just the right words. Oh, to have all the perfect expressions of love in his mind, just waiting to be said.

Instead of rising to the occasion, forcing himself to conjure up a magical phrase or two, Zachary felt drained, as if he no longer could hold himself up. Did that dull side of his personality bother Nori as well? She had every right to worry about marrying a man who was as exciting as an empty jar of jelly.

"I just don't want us to rush into anything," Nori said after a long pause. "What if we were to make an error in judgment? You know. . .do something we'd both regret all our lives. We don't even know the basics about each other."

"What do you mean?"

Nori seemed to study him. "Like for instance, what's my favorite color?"

"Well, I think you can know people's characters and essences without knowing their favorite colors." Zachary didn't want to manipulate or make light of her doubts, yet he still found himself wanting to defend his love.

"See, you don't know what my—"

"Lavender." Zachary leaned over the railing, looking away from her. "Your favorite color is lavender."

"But how could you—"

"You wear that color twice as often as any other color. So I assumed it's your favorite." He laced his fingers together but didn't glance back at her.

"I wear lavender twice as often? How could you know that? *I* didn't even know that." She reached out and touched Zachary's cheek. "That is very sweet of you to notice, though."

Nori called me sweet. Not a good sign—probably what women say when they're trying to say good-bye. For the last time. Should he make the moment less painful for her by letting her walk away? Or should he keep trying to persuade her of his devotion? Even when she was frightened of the consequences? Was he being noble or selfish? Perhaps he would never deserve such delight. *God, please help me.*

Zachary waded through the awkward moment, but not without some perspiration and prayer. Then he decided to try and rescue the moment. "I may not know a lot about you, but I feel I know the important things." He looked straight into her eyes. "You have a kind face and a generous spirit. I love many of the same things you do, and we both love and worship the one true God. I know we come at life from different angles, but that's the beauty of it. We're like this prism. When the light hits it, colors stream out of it. . .separate and yet flowing together as one." He shut up then and wondered how he'd gotten himself to say such words.

"That was by far the most beautiful thing any man has ever said to me. Or will *ever* say to me." She chuckled. "You're making this so hard. I'm trying to set you free if that's what you need, and here you—"

"It's not what I need. Or want." Zachary took her by the shoulders. "Without you, I'd be lonely and miserable in Denver. But what about you? Can you let go of what we have that easily?"

She shook her head. "No. I think there'd always be a hole there. A place you filled that no one else can fill. There's no doubt I'd be a little lost."

"Only a little?"

"I don't know." Nori pulled away from him. "But even if I *did* know for sure how I felt, our choices are still pretty bleak. Quitting your job is not a good option. And if we dated, flying back and forth would be very hard. If we ever *did* marry, then I'd be forced to sell my shop. You see, even though my grandmother wasn't a wealthy woman, she insisted on giving me the money to start Sweet Nothings. She trusted me to follow my dream. The shop is finally taking off. I just can't walk away from the sacrifice she made. It wouldn't be fair to her."

"No, of course not." Zachary dropped his gaze. "I would never ask you to sell your business."

Nori's eyes filled with tears.

He felt terrible that he'd put that sadness in her face. He pulled out a handkerchief from his jacket pocket and dabbed at the wetness on her cheeks. "I'm sorry I made you cry."

"You know, I think I believe you now," she said in a soft voice. "You really *do* love me."

"Yes." Zachary lifted her chin.

Nori shook her head. "Why is the timing in life always so off? Why is everything that is good and right always so hard?" She took his hand and placed it against her cheek. "I like what we have together. I don't want to lose it. And yet, there seems to be this great and impossible fissure. . .where there's no bridge."

There was so much more Zachary wanted to say, but now perhaps it was pointless. Nori had made up her mind, and he would not continue to badger her or make her cry.

"When would you have to go?" she asked.

Her words jarred him back to reality. "The company moves everything in about six weeks." He winced. "But now. . .I guess I'll catch a flight out this afternoon and search for an apartment."

Nori's cell phone came to life in her purse. "I'm so sorry." She looked at the caller. "It's my father. I'd better take it. I'm sorry."

"It's okay. Go ahead." Zachary sat on the bench away from her, wanting to give her some privacy. He watched her from a distance as she answered the phone.

Nori held her finger over her other ear. She seemed to listen for a few minutes, frowning and sighing. It became obvious whatever her father was saying to her caused her pain. After a few more minutes, Nori folded up her phone and walked back to him. "It's my father, finally responding to my messages."

"You're upset. Do you want to sit for a while and tell me what's wrong?"

Nori sat down close to him. "He called to tell me the divorce is almost final. He said Mom mentioned something about possibly marrying someone else. And he's okay with that. I can't believe it." She placed her hand over her mouth.

"I'm so sorry." Zachary put his arm around her.

She rested her head against his shoulder but said no more.

What an awful blow for Nori. He spent the quiet in prayer for her. But in the midst of his appeal to God, he became aware of his own sorrow, since as self-seeking as the thought seemed, he knew this latest misfortune would affect his life as well.

Surely his chances of wooing Nori were over.

twenty-three

Nori wasn't sure how long she'd been sitting on her couch in her bathrobe, just staring at the wall. Minutes, maybe an hour. She did feel badly, though, for leaving the store so early in the morning. But after she'd burst into tears, Lizza had insisted she go home to rest.

Oh great. Was that someone at the door? She slogged to the door and opened it. Her mother stood in the hallway, looking misplaced. "Mother?"

"Hi." She shuffled her feet. "Will you let me in?"

"Of course." Dad must have told her about his phone call. *So, Mom knows I know about her possible marriage.*

This time Nori was pulled into a warm hug by her mother. The exchange felt good. Comforting. And long overdue.

"May I have some of that famous hot chocolate of yours?" her mother asked as she headed toward the kitchen.

"Sure." Nori followed behind her, wondering what she was going to say. And praying her own words wouldn't get too sharp or divisive.

They puttered around the kitchen together, gathering up the turbinado sugar, the unsweetened chocolate, and the milk and cream. When the cocoa was ready, Nori poured it into mugs and then garnished it with peppermint sticks and dollops of homemade whipped cream.

They both sat down and took careful sips.

Her mother dabbed at the whipped cream mustache on her upper lip. "This is good."

"Thanks."

"I suppose you know why I came."

"Well, Dad finally called me back."

Her mother fiddled with her napkin, folding it and unfolding it. "Well, I didn't tell you about the possibility of remarrying since it didn't seem necessary at the time."

"I love you. I'm your *daughter*. I would want to know."

"Yes, I see that now. Leaving for a cruise was silly. I felt like such a sneak that morning. Anyway, I ended up canceling my trip."

"Oh?" Nori wondered why she wasn't told. Why such mystery? She realized she didn't know her mother. Perhaps she never had.

"I want you to go ahead with your questions now." Somber creases lined her mother's face. "The ones you never got to ask."

"All right." Nori took in a deep breath, relieved for the chance to understand. "So, *you* asked for the divorce because you want to marry another man." She kept her tone respectful.

"Well, yes, I brought up the subject of divorce with your father, but he readily agreed to it."

"Really?" Nori looked down at her fingers, which had balled up into fists.

"Yes." Her mother licked her lips. "But there is something else you need to know."

Oh no. Can I handle more surprises? "Okay."

"Well, I need to just get this out." She shook her head. "Before I married your father, I was in love with a man named Roger Conley."

Nori gave her a smile, but inside she already felt weary of the discussion. "Then why didn't you marry Roger?"

Her mother pursed her lips. "Because my mother demanded that I marry your father. I didn't want to, but I had no say in the matter."

"But Grandma Essie was so sweet. I can't imagine her doing such—"

"She was sweet to *you*. She adored you, in fact. But she was quite the spitfire in her younger days, and she did a pretty good job of controlling my life."

"But why would Grandma Essie do that? Force you and Dad to marry?" Nori hugged her middle for support. She couldn't stand to think of her beloved grandmother doing anything so deplorable.

"She made us marry right away. . .because your father and I were going to have a baby."

Nori blinked a few times. "Me?"

Her mother nodded.

Okay, stay calm, Nori. She tried to steady her breathing.

Her mother scooted her chair closer to her. "Please understand. We'd made a terrible mistake. I know that."

"*I* was a mistake?"

"I'm not trying to say *you* were a mistake." She pushed her hair away from her face. "Surely you understand what I mean. It's just—"

"But why isn't Roger my father. . .if you loved him?" Nori realized her question might be getting too intimate. "You don't have to answer that."

"Thank you for not demanding an answer. You do have a right to know, but it's kind of complicated. And to be honest, after all these years, it's kind of hazy, too. Anyway, my mother wanted us to do the right thing, but marrying the wrong man just piled one mistake on top of another."

Nori wasn't sure what to say now. All her talks on devotion seemed diluted by the truth. God didn't like divorce, and yet He wouldn't force people into marriage. Confusion clouded her reason and resolve.

Perhaps she'd feel a little better if her mother stroked her hair and whispered to her that all would be well. Isn't that what mothers always did? Yet Nori couldn't even summon a single memory of her mother comforting her in such a way.

"Your father is okay with this decision. He's not hurting."

"But *I'm* hurting." Nori rose and splayed her fingers on the table. "Doesn't that mean anything?" She knew her words were selfish and insensitive, but the words still flowed out of her. *God, am I lashing out in pain or reprisal?*

"Of course it matters what you think. But in the end, I have to live my own life. I can't always be living it the way others want me to. That's what I did for my mother, and it didn't work." She reached out to Nori and clung to her arm. "I have a little time left for happiness. My mother snatched this joy from me. Please don't let it be my own daughter who keeps it from me when I have a second chance." Her voice became raspy. "I think that would be too ironic for this old heart to take."

"But. . .what does God want in all this?" Nori touched her mother's hand, which still clung to her arm.

"To be honest, dear, I haven't asked Him. I haven't been close to Him for a while now." She let out a long puff of air. "By now, I think maybe He's forgotten about me."

"That's not the nature of God. . .to forget. He could honor this commitment you've kept with Dad by giving you love. . . if only you'd ask Him."

"That's sweet, Nori, but isn't it kind of naive?" She released her arm.

"Anything is possible with God."

Her mother took another mouthful of hot chocolate and then looked at her intently. "I want you to know something. There's been no infidelity in our marriage. Your father and I have been faithful all these years. Do you understand?"

"I do."

"And someday when you marry, if you choose to marry, promise me you'll marry for love."

"I will." Nori dipped her head, feeling so many emotions that she wasn't sure what to deal with first. But when she saw the lifeless and remorse-filled expression on her mother's face, it tore at her heart. "I'm sorry it was me who got in the way of the man you really loved."

Her mother gave her a firm nod. "It's not your fault." She rose and rubbed her hands along the counter. "Although there was a time when I felt differently. And I've always wanted to talk to you about that."

"Oh?" Nori wondered what she could mean.

"When you were growing up, I think I resented you from time to time. Whenever I got to thinking about Roger and what could have been, well, somehow in the midst of thinking about my predicament I forgot how to be a good mother."

Nori stared at her hands, which were folded in her lap. "But what did—"

She put her hand up. "Please let me get all the way through this. I need to say these things. I've practiced this speech for years." She cleared her throat. "What I'm trying to apologize for is the way I treated you sometimes. I was too hard on you. You know, the way I made you do things over and over when you were little."

"Over and over?" Nori asked. "What do you mean?"

"Well, sometimes when I was upset about my circumstances, I would take my irritation out on you by telling you that you weren't doing things right." She ground her knuckles into the counter. "You'd make your little bed and then I'd come behind you and undo it, saying you didn't do it right. Or you'd make a stack of folded towels, and I'd knock them over and make you start again. Those kinds of things." She looked away. "I'm sure you know what I mean."

Nori searched her mind, and then one by one, some of the hurtful moments her mother spoke of came filtering back. She winced and hugged herself. "Yes. I guess I do remember a little now." Perhaps she'd blocked some of the memories since they were so painful.

"I guess they were acts of retaliation. But it was cruel to take out my frustration on an innocent child. *My* child. I can't believe I did the things I did. I'm so sorry." She brought her fists up to her forehead.

Like a lens adjusting its focus, Nori began to see why she'd grown up with compulsive behaviors. Somehow knowing, just knowing the truth, was a great relief.

Her mother turned to her. "Nori, please, will you ever forgive me?"

Nori rushed into her mother's arms. "Yes, I do. I forgive you."

They hugged for some time as a quiet reverence settled over them.

"You know what I've wanted over the years?" Her mother whispered into her hair. "Even more than Roger?"

"What?" Nori asked.

"This moment. When I could finally get myself to say those things. And then to hear you say that you'd forgiven me. It takes courage to admit such embarrassing things, and I've been a coward for a long time."

Nori could no longer hold back the tears. "I love you, Mom. I always have."

"And you're my greatest blessing in this life." She moved from the embrace and leaned against the counter, her eyes flooding with fresh tears. She waved her hands in frustration. "And here I was determined to get through this without crying." She raised her hands. "It's impossible."

Nori smiled. "I don't mind." She thought her mother had never looked so beautiful. And her hug never felt so comforting.

"Okay, so that I don't turn into a total fool here, why don't you tell me something happy? Something wonderful in your delicious, candy-filled life."

Nori knew this might not be the best time to tell her mother about Zachary, yet she felt compelled to continue their newfound camaraderie. "I *do* have something to tell you. . . ."

Her mother sat down. "Please tell me."

Nori laced her fingers together. "A man proposed to me today," she said in an excited whisper.

"What? Really?"

"Hey, don't act so surprised." Nori grinned.

Her mother chuckled. "I'm only surprised because I didn't even know you were dating anyone."

"Well, I haven't said yes. I wanted to give it some time."

"Do you love him?"

Nori released a puff of air. "I believe I do. But I'm a little scared."

"Well, you already know what my advice would be. Only marry him if you're sure." Her mother leaned toward her. "What's he like?"

"He's an exceptional man, smart and handsome. A wonderfully kind Christian man. I don't deserve him, but he loves me."

"Oh my. He sounds remarkable."

Nori clasped her fingers together. "He is."

She gathered her daughter's hands in hers. "I have one more word of advice. Do you want to hear it?"

"Yes, please."

"I don't want our divorce to scare you away from marriage. That would be the worst kind of torture for me. Do you understand? If you love him and this is meant to be, I'd hate to see you forgo your happiness because of what's happening between your father and me."

"Okay." Nori took a long drink of her cocoa. "And will you do one thing for me?"

"I'll try."

"Before the divorce is final, will you ask God about it? Just talk to Him about it. That's all I'm asking."

Her mother paused. "That's a hard one, Nori. But I give you my word." She grinned. "Now, please tell me more about this young man of yours."

Nori chuckled. "Sure."

After an hour of heart-sharing and a bite of lunch, her mother left with a promise to stay in touch.

Nori shut the door still wishing her mother would change her mind about the divorce, and yet her heart overflowed with gratitude for the forgiveness that had started a healing in their relationship. It had been a merciful gift from God and one she hadn't even asked for. In fact, perhaps she hadn't asked for the Lord's help often enough. Maybe God was trying to give her an answer about marrying Zachary and she was too busy to hear Him.

That still, small voice. Nori sighed. Had she taken the time to really listen? It was easy to forget that the Lord wanted to brighten every corner and crevice of her life—the already radiant stuff, the shadowy stuff, and the dark stuff. Had she forgotten how dazzling and piercing and calming His light really was? *One way to find out.*

She remembered the new prayer chapel their congregation had just completed and decided to make use of it. Nori drove up to her church and parked near the stone walkway that led to The Chapel in the Woods. She strolled down the winding path through the stand of pines and gazed up at the building. The chapel had a quaint look to it, complete with a tiny steeple, an arched front door, and several stained-glass windows.

Nori tried the lever on the door handle. *Open. Perfect.* She headed down the aisle, passing by the short rows of wooden pews, and then sat down in the front row. As she took in the beauty of the chapel, her gaze traveled over the vaulted ceiling and beams, the beautifully carved altar, and the magnificent stained-glass window just in front of her. The glowing glass depicted Christ listening to a group of children who were gathered at His feet.

Her hands folded together as she meditated on the scene, wondering what the Lord would have said to the little ones who wanted nothing more than to be near Him. And how would the children have responded to His words? They must have felt safe enough to share their stories with Him. Yes, Jesus always was a good listener.

Still is, a voice echoed in her mind.

Nori knelt at the altar. Without holding anything back, she poured out her heart like a child—emptying all the joys and worries and hopes to her Father, her Friend, and her Savior.

After a long moment of reflection and then a prompting in her spirit, she prayed. "Forgive me, Lord, for desiring that tight little circle of love to always be about romance and not about You. I acknowledge You as the Lover of my soul and the Someone who cares for me far more than any husband ever could. Help me never to forget these truths and to love You first, above all."

And then Nori wept. And waited. And listened. The Lord came near and comforted her. After some time had passed, she rose from the bench, feeling refreshed.

Nori walked out of the chapel with peace and an answer to the happy dilemma bursting in her heart. She would marry the man she dearly loved and move with him to Denver. She felt certain Lizza would buy the shop, and then all would be well. Zachary wouldn't have to quit his job, and she could start a new Sweet Nothings in Denver.

Once back at the apartment building, she rang Zachary's doorbell, hoping she could catch him before he headed to the airport. She paused for a moment and then rang the bell again. Nothing. Nori looked at her watch. 4:05 p.m. He'd already gone.

After a long wait with no response, Nori glanced up and down the hallway, wondering what to do next.

At that moment, Ivan the Not-So-Great emerged from his apartment.

"Ivan, have you seen Zachary?"

"Who?"

"Zachary Martin. You know. . .the guy who lives right next to me."

"Oh, you mean the geek you're dating?"

Nori winced. "Please don't say that."

Ivan looked hopeful. "So, you're *not* dating him anymore?"

"No, I mean please don't call Zachary a geek."

"Why not?"

"Because he's a wonderful man, and I'm in love with him." Nori surprised herself, saying those words, and yet she knew it was the truth.

Ivan pulled back. "Is that right? You love him?"

"Yep. That's right. So, have you seen Zachary?"

"Yeah."

Nori breathed a prayer of thanksgiving. "Where and when?"

"Well, I saw him this morning when we all got on the elevator together."

Her shoulders drooped. "No, I mean since then."

Ivan nodded. "Yeah, I did see him come back home."

"When was it? Did he leave again? Did he have any luggage with him?"

Ivan held up his hand. "Hold on. I'm trying."

"Sorry."

"He came home maybe ten minutes ago. But I don't know if he went out again. He did have a piece of luggage with him. I'm sure of that. One carry-on bag."

"Did he say anything?"

Ivan shook his head. "No."

"Did he look upset. . .at all?"

"Sorry, I wasn't paying much attention. Is everything okay?"

Nori took in a deep breath. "I'm going to make it okay. If I can."

"Good luck then." He smiled.

"Thanks. I appreciate your help."

"Sure." Ivan gave her a wave and went on his way.

Nori heaved a sigh of relief, thinking Zachary must not have gone to Denver after all. He'd changed his mind. But why wasn't he answering his door? Had he seen her through the peephole and then refused to let her in? Did he think she wasn't worth so much indecision and doubt? The flood of new concerns didn't win her over. Zachary's devotion appeared real and lasting. His love wouldn't be so easily discarded.

Nevertheless, Nori felt a need for some serious haste. Perhaps she still had time to make things right. She'd call Lizza at work and discuss the sale of Sweet Nothings. Then she'd give Zachary's door another sound rap. Surely her news of commitment would convince him of her love.

Determination mingled with her excitement as she swung open her front door and raced to the phone.

twenty-four

Zachary unplugged his coffee grinder. *Wow, that stupid machine is loud.* Had he heard somebody at the door while he was grinding his bag of coffee? He listened. Nothing. Must have been noise from upstairs. He often heard pounding as if somebody up there was learning to step dance—somebody, in fact, who was a kinsman to Goliath.

With robotic efforts and zero enthusiasm, he cleaned out the coffee grinder, put the grounds away in a large glass container, and then decided not to make coffee after all. Caffeine wasn't going to make him feel any better. What he really wanted to do was bang his head against the wall, but he knew the act would prove itself too infantile and unproductive as well as painful. But what could be worse than the way he felt now?

He plopped on his couch and didn't move. His flight to Denver had just left, but all his inspiring self-talk wasn't enough to get him on that plane. What would happen now? He'd have to schedule another flight. But then the love of his life wouldn't be a part of his future. He had envisioned so many good things with Nori. Taking her to the jazz festival. Hiking all the trails together in the national park. Sharing their first Christmas.

What a disaster. How had he come to know such misery? He hadn't moved to the apartment with the idea of finding someone to love. But now there was no second guessing. No turning back. He'd have to live with the lonely truth. Love happened, and there was nothing he could do about it but suffer.

Zachary rested his head in his palms. If Nori was never meant to love him, then he must have taken a wrong turn somewhere. *But where?* Hadn't he prayed about the situation and felt a peace about it? Hadn't he gotten the green light? Maybe he was color-blind.

Zachary squeezed his temples. If only Nori's parents had waited to talk about their divorce. . . He and Nori could have married before the fallout. But then there was always the possibility she would have regretted marrying him, and that would have hurt even more.

Then a new scenario hit Zachary. Maybe there was more at play than the breakup of Nori's parents. Maybe Nori had other reasons for wanting to sever their connection. Perhaps he'd poured his compulsive behavior into their budding affections like motor oil into leaded crystal and Nori had decided one person with OCD was more than enough.

God, if I messed up somewhere, could You please undo my mistakes? Clear the file? Is there anyway I can have another chance?

He groaned, thinking of the worst possibility of all. "Lord, even though it's painful for me to even think of the other possibility. . .I still want Your will. If Nori was never meant to be my wife, then please help me to let her go."

Tears wet his skin, and he brushed them away. As he sat there, though, an idea formed. Maybe Nori was so focused on the fear of divorce that what she needed most from him was a sign of devotion and commitment. But how could he accomplish that?

Zachary rose off the couch. *I will quit my job, even without the promise of another.* He could always consider other career options, but he needed to stay in Hot Springs. That would prove to Nori he wasn't about to toss her off easily. That's what she needed. . .right? To know that he was determined and faithful and willing to sacrifice everything for her?

Zachary dropped back down on the couch in confusion. *And the whole plan could backfire on me. Big time.* Giving up his job could upset her. She might think he'd been foolhardy and impulsive in not talking to her first. That he'd presumed on their affections, and that he'd pressured her by taking such a drastic step.

He imagined himself sitting on the couch for the rest of his days, alone, without Nori. Unbearable. But was this new idea a prompting from God, or was it the pathetic ruminations of a desperate man? Unless the Almighty was going to come forth with some Old Testament–style writing on the wall as a definitive answer, then he just might have to go forth in faith and pray that the Lord would take care of the rest.

With renewed resolve and a sudden injection of calm in his spirit, he constructed a letter of resignation on his computer, printed it out, and headed toward the door.

twenty-five

Nori hung up the phone. Just as she'd guessed, Lizza was happy to buy Sweet Nothings and overjoyed to learn why the shop was for sale.

She hurried back to Zachary's apartment and rang his bell. Nori caught herself giggling, imagining his face as she announced the sale of her shop. She placed her hand over her heart. *So this is what it feels like to be in love.*

Zachary didn't come to the door, so she mashed the bell a few more times. Maybe she'd taken too much time working out the details with Lizza. Was he still refusing to answer his door, or had he just left for the airport? What a comedy of errors, except the situation was far from funny!

Tears started to fill her eyes. *Stay calm, Nori.* Then an idea came to her. Surely someone at South Gate Oil and Gas would know his plans. She glanced at her watch. 4:45. They hadn't shut down for the day, so there was still time to call. After getting the number from Information, she quickly pushed in all the right buttons.

Nori counted each second as she waited for a receptionist to answer. Even though the passing of time hadn't altered, this was starting to feel like the longest day of her life. She drummed her fingers on the kitchen counter.

"Good afternoon. South Gate Oil and Gas. May I help you?"

Finally, a human being. Thank You, Lord. "I'm looking for Zachary Martin. Please."

"Mr. Zachary Martin?" a young woman's voice said.

"Yes. That's correct."

"Well, I think I saw Mr. Martin leaving the building maybe five minutes ago. Let me check on that for you. One moment please."

The woman placed her on hold. Nori waited, drumming her fingers.

"Yes, I was correct," the woman finally said. "Mr. Martin just left. I don't—"

"Was he leaving for Denver?" Nori tried to keep her voice in a normal vocal range, but she knew it was getting higher-pitched by the second.

"No, Mr. Martin no longer works here."

"Oh no." Nori's heart sank. "Are you absolutely sure?"

"From what I just heard, he won't be making the move with our company. He quit his job."

Nori clutched her throat. "I can't believe it."

"Well, I can," the girl said. "Just between you and me, some other people have quit, too. Some people just don't want to make the move."

"Thank you for your help," Nori said. "Oh, did he say where he was going?"

"You mean what kind of job—"

"No, I mean if he was headed home right now or some-where else?"

"Sorry, I don't have that information. No, wait. He did say something about a favorite spot. But I don't know where that is."

"I do. Thanks for your help." Nori put the phone back. *This is my fault. That dear sweet man is out of work because of me.* She couldn't contain her anguish as tears spilled down her cheeks. She wiped them away. At least she knew where Zachary had gone.

Nori drove as quickly as she could without killing anyone, found a parking place, and headed up the stairs, which over-looked the cascades.

There was Zachary, just sitting on a bench and looking like the most dejected man on earth. "How could I do this to you?" she murmured. She breathed a prayer for courage and walked over to him.

Zachary looked up, surprised and very pleased. "You've come."

Nori sat down next to him. She wasn't sure what to say first. So much needed to be said. "I heard you quit your job. Why?"

"This place is home, and you're part of that. At least I hope this will allow us to continue to date. I want to give you all the time you need, Nori." He looked at her. "I'll find work. Somehow."

Zachary's earnestness ripped at her heart. "But I hadn't even said yes. I mean. . .that was taking quite a chance."

"I guess that's what love does."

Nori wanted to kiss that despair right off his face, but the time wasn't right. Not until she'd said what she needed to say. "You know, Lizza loves my shop, and the customers adore her. I just talked to her, and she's going to buy Sweet Nothings so I can start over in Denver. Maybe if you hurry, you can get your job back."

"No." Zachary rose, looking troubled. "You can't sell your shop."

"My love for you is more important than any company. And you were right. I got so caught up in the whirlwind of my parents' troubles, it kept me from seeing what was right in front of me. But I see it all clearly now." Nori placed her hand over her mouth, feeling choked with emotion. "How can this be?"

Zachary eased down next to her. "How can what be, Nori?"

"That I could be so fortunate. . .that you would love me. I've prayed a thousand prayers for a man to come along just like you. And there you were all this time. God must have one incredible sense of humor." Nori chuckled through her tears. "But He also has mercy. He remembered my prayers all these years, and He gave me you, Zachary Martin. You are the present I want to open before it's too late."

Zachary's eyes misted over. "It's not too late."

Nori loved his passion. She loved *him*. Pure and simple. And now she had some proposing to do. "I have something else I want to say." She knelt down on one knee in front of Zachary. "You asked me a question here, and I turned you down. Well, now *I'm* asking." She took his hands in hers. And while jets thundered overhead and tourists ambled by, Nori said, "Mr. Martin, I once saved your life. Now would you please save mine?" She kissed his hand and smiled. "Would you do me the honor of becoming my husband?"

Zachary rose and lifted her into his arms. "Oh, how I love you, my dearest Irish maiden. The answer is categorically affirmative."

Nori laughed, thinking she'd never felt so wonderful or seen Zachary so happy. Then he kissed her—a real kiss. A big juicy one. The very one, in fact, she'd dared to ask God for. And it was a kiss that meant something. Something real and lasting. A forever kind of kiss.

twenty-six

Seven months later

Lizza helped slip the ivory Victorian gown over Nori's head. If there was such a thing as bridal rapture, Nori definitely had it. *I'm getting married.* Finally—after years of hoping, praying, believing—she would walk down the aisle on her father's arm.

Lizza stepped behind Nori and zipped up the delicate dress, then fussed with the lengthy beaded train. Her best friend's hand went to her mouth as she stood back. "You're the most beautiful bride I've ever seen. And I'm not just saying that."

"Sure you're not." Nori chuckled and then turned to look at herself in the mirror. For a moment, the reflection took her breath away. She looked—and felt—like a princess. Just as she'd always dreamed. She ran her fingers along the delicate Chantilly lace.

Right away, she thought of the wedding doll her mother had given her on her sixth birthday. How many years had she played with that exquisite little doll, imagining the wedding she would one day have? And how many different types of ceremonies had she planned? Hundreds.

Oh, but today's would be the best of all. Not just because of its classic traditional style but because the man waiting for her at the front of the church was Zachary—*her* Zachary.

Nori couldn't help but smile as she thought of her groom. What was he doing right now? Fumbling with his bow tie, no doubt, reflecting on how much it reminded him of the magnetic field of the earth. She grinned at that thought. And maybe Zachary was sending another prayer of thanksgiving for his new job in Hot Springs as a geophysical consultant.

A rap on the door interrupted her reverie, and Nori glanced over as her mother entered the room with a black box in hand. "This is the pearl necklace I showed you a few months ago. It belonged to your great-grandmother, your grandmother, and then to me." She opened the box. "But now they are my gift to you."

"Oh Mom, are you sure?" She bit her lip and forced back the tears.

"Very sure." Her mother placed the strand of pearls around Nori's neck.

"They're exquisite. Thank you so much."

They hugged each other, and her mother began to cry. Despite her best efforts, Nori quickly followed.

"None of that, you two." Lizza shook her finger at them and grinned. "Your makeup will melt like cotton candy!"

Nori chuckled and reached for a tissue. How she loved her dear friend and now business partner. She was thrilled that Lizza was about to open Sweet Nothings II in Little Rock. Lizza would have her own shop after all. What a blessing for everyone.

Lizza lifted the headdress of silk blossoms off the stand and carefully pinned it to Nori's upswept curls. She stepped back and straightened the beaded tulle as it cascaded down Nori's back, completing the picture. "Mmm. Like icing on the cake."

"Look at this. All grown-up." Her mother dabbed at her eyes. "I just can't believe it. My little girl is about to get married."

Nori gave her mother an inviting smile, feeling so very blessed that her parents hadn't signed the divorce papers after all but had decided to get marriage counseling instead.

"Oh, how I love you," her mother whispered to her.

Nori basked in the wonder of her loving words. "I love you, too."

Another knock on the door caused the ladies to turn in curiosity. A tentative male voice rang out. "C–can I come in?"

Dad! A knot rose in Nori's throat as her father stepped into the room. He took one look at her and reached to take her hand, tears slipping down his cheeks.

Nori looked back and forth between her parents and ushered up a silent prayer. *Oh Lord, thank You that they're both here for me.*

She turned to face her father and gave his hand a squeeze. "It's okay, Dad. I'm sure by the time this day is over we'll all be drying our eyes. I know I will be."

Lizza, still playing the role of organizer, handed out bouquets of red roses, each framed with greenery. They looked beautiful against the emerald green bridesmaids' dresses.

With joy overflowing, Nori took her Bible in hand, the same one that had guided her through her relationship with Zachary. Affixed to the front of the Bible was a spray of bridal pink roses. Nori pulled them to her face at once to inhale their fragrance. Then she looked at the special bouquet of bridal pink roses that had just arrived. Zachary had sent them. He'd remembered they were her favorite. She'd memorized his attached card.

To my Irish maiden,
All of nature comes to life
And celebrates our delight
As we walk, so full of love
In our fields of amber light.

Ah, Zachary. He really did have a poet's heart. And he'd sent her a box of her favorite candies—lavender chocolate truffles from Belgium. He'd thought of everything.

Suddenly the familiar strains of Pachelbel's *Canon in D* drew Nori's attention to the open door that led to the sanctuary.

"I think that's our cue." Her father extended his arm to her. "Are you ready?"

"Oh, I am *so* ready." She gave herself one last glance in the mirror and then paused, remembering something. "Oh, just a second." Reaching into her beaded purse, she came up with a container of pomegranate lipstick, which she applied with care.

Funny how Zachary had fallen in love with the color during the months of their engagement. Funnier still as she realized the external changes they'd both made had nothing to do with their blossoming love for one another.

With Lizza, her maid of honor, and then her bridesmaids leading the procession, they all made their way down the hallway toward the back of the familiar church sanctuary. The doors swept open, and for the first time all day, she set her sights on her bridegroom.

Oh my. Zachary looked every bit like a prince in his tuxedo and silk vest. Okay, so his tie was a little askew and his hair stuck out a bit on one side, but his face lit up with expectancy, and all the more so when he caught a glimpse of her. Love poured from his eyes, and Nori fought to keep the tears from flowing.

The organist shifted with dramatic flair to the triumphant bridal march, and Nori's heart thumped in anticipation. She squeezed her father's arm, knowing the moment had come at last—the one she had dreamed of since childhood. The pipe organ seemed to beckon, wooing her to the front of the church.

"Are you ready?" her father whispered.

"Oh yes."

She took the first nerve-racking step with her right foot. Then her left. Then her right. Somewhere along the way, she and her father entered into a steady gait, walking in time with the music. They reached the altar area in record time, and Nori smiled as Zachary looked her way and mouthed a silent, "I love you."

Nori responded with a nod. Of course, the tears got in the way, but she didn't mind as she took her place next to Zachary. *Ahh.* The world was suddenly a much finer place. So fine, in fact, that Nori thought no confection on earth could ever be as sweet.

A Letter To Our Readers

Dear Reader:

In order that we might better contribute to your reading enjoyment, we would appreciate your taking a few minutes to respond to the following questions. We welcome your comments and read each form and letter we receive. When completed, please return to the following:

Fiction Editor
Heartsong Presents
PO Box 719
Uhrichsville, Ohio 44683

1. Did you enjoy reading *Castles in the Air* by Anita Higman and Janice A. Thompson?
   ❏ Very much! I would like to see more books by this author!
   ❏ Moderately. I would have enjoyed it more if

   _____

   _____

   _____

2. Are you a member of **Heartsong Presents**? ❏ Yes ❏ No
   If no, where did you purchase this book? _____

   _____

3. How would you rate, on a scale from 1 (poor) to 5 (superior), the cover design? _____

4. On a scale from 1 (poor) to 10 (superior), please rate the following elements.

   ____ Heroine   ____ Plot
   ____ Hero   ____ Inspirational theme
   ____ Setting   ____ Secondary characters

5. These characters were special because? _____
_____
_____

6. How has this book inspired your life? _____
_____
_____

7. What settings would you like to see covered in future
   Heartsong Presents books? _____
_____
_____

8. What are some inspirational themes you would like to see
   treated in future books? _____
_____
_____

9. Would you be interested in reading other **Heartsong
   Presents** titles? ❏ Yes   ❏ No

10. Please check your age range:
    ❏ Under 18   ❏ 18-24
    ❏ 25-34   ❏ 35-45
    ❏ 46-55   ❏ Over 55

Name _____
Occupation _____
Address _____
City, State, Zip _____

Heart♥ng

Any 12 Heartsong Presents titles for only $27.00*

CONTEMPORARY ROMANCE IS CHEAPER BY THE DOZEN!

Buy any assortment of twelve *Heartsong Presents* titles and save 25% off the already discounted price of $2.97 each!

*plus $4.00 shipping and handling per order and sales tax where applicable. If outside the U.S. please call 740-922-7280 for shipping charges.

HEARTSONG PRESENTS TITLES AVAILABLE NOW:

___HP546 *Love Is Kind*, J. Livingston
___HP549 *Patchwork and Politics*, C. Lynxwiler
___HP550 *Woodhaven Acres*, B. Etchison
___HP553 *Bay Island*, B. Loughner
___HP554 *A Donut a Day*, G. Sattler
___HP557 *If You Please*, T. Davis
___HP558 *A Fairy Tale Romance*, M. Panagiotopoulos
___HP561 *Ton's Vow*, K. Cornelius
___HP562 *Family Ties*, J. L. Barton
___HP565 *An Unbreakable Hope*, K. Billerbeck
___HP566 *The Baby Quilt*, J. Livingston
___HP569 *Ageless Love*, L. Bliss
___HP570 *Beguiling Masquerade*, C. G. Page
___HP573 *In a Land Far Far Away*, M. Panagiotopoulos
___HP574 *Lambert's Pride*, L. A. Coleman and R. Hauck
___HP577 *Anita's Fortune*, K. Cornelius
___HP578 *The Birthday Wish*, J. Livingston
___HP581 *Love Online*, K. Billerbeck
___HP582 *The Long Ride Home*, A. Boeshaar
___HP585 *Compassion's Charm*, D. Mills
___HP586 *A Single Rose*, P. Griffin
___HP589 *Changing Seasons*, C. Reece and J. Reece-Demarco
___HP590 *Secret Admirer*, G. Sattler
___HP593 *Angel Incognito*, J. Thompson
___HP594 *Out on a Limb*, G. Gaymer Martin
___HP597 *Let My Heart Go*, B. Huston
___HP598 *More Than Friends*, T. H. Murray
___HP601 *Timing is Everything*, T. V. Bateman
___HP602 *Dandelion Bride*, J. Livingston
___HP605 *Picture Imperfect*, N. J. Farrier
___HP606 *Mary's Choice*, Kay Cornelius
___HP609 *Through the Fire*, C. Lynxwiler
___HP613 *Chorus of One*, J. Thompson
___HP614 *Forever in My Heart*, L. Ford
___HP617 *Run Fast, My Love*, P. Griffin

___HP618 *One Last Christmas*, J. Livingston
___HP621 *Forever Friends*, T. H. Murray
___HP622 *Time Will Tell*, L. Bliss
___HP625 *Love's Image*, D. Mayne
___HP626 *Down From the Cross*, J. Livingston
___HP629 *Look to the Heart*, T. Fowler
___HP630 *The Flat Marriage Fix*, K. Hayse
___HP633 *Longing for Home*, C. Lynxwiler
___HP634 *The Child Is Mine*, M. Colvin
___HP637 *Mother's Day*, J. Livingston
___HP638 *Real Treasure*, T. Davis
___HP641 *The Pastor's Assignment*, K. O'Brien
___HP642 *What's Cooking*, G. Sattler
___HP645 *The Hunt for Home*, G. Aiken
___HP649 *4th of July*, J. Livingston
___HP650 *Romanian Rhapsody*, D. Franklin
___HP653 *Lakeside*, M. Davis
___HP654 *Alaska Summer*, M. H. Flinkman
___HP657 *Love Worth Finding*, C. M. Hake
___HP658 *Love Worth Keeping*, J. Livingston
___HP661 *Lambert's Code*, R. Hauck
___HP665 *Bah Humbug, Mrs. Scrooge*, J. Livingston
___HP666 *Sweet Charity*, J. Thompson
___HP669 *The Island*, M. Davis
___HP670 *Miss Menace*, N. Lavo
___HP673 *Flash Flood*, D. Mills
___HP677 *Banking on Love*, J. Thompson
___HP678 *Lambert's Peace*, R. Hauck
___HP681 *The Wish*, L. Bliss
___HP682 *The Grand Hotel*, M. Davis
___HP685 *Thunder Bay*, B. Loughner
___HP686 *Always a Bridesmaid*, A. Boeshaar
___HP689 *Unforgettable*, J. L. Barton
___HP690 *Heritage*, M. Davis
___HP693 *Dear John*, K. V. Sawyer
___HP694 *Riches of the Heart*, T. Davis
___HP697 *Dear Granny*, P. Griffin
___HP698 *With a Mother's Heart*, J. Livingston

(If ordering from this page, please remember to include it with the order form.)